Seismic Eruptions

By

Jenny Ahmed

Other Books by Jenny Ahmed:

All the King's Men

By Dawn's Early Light

The Burning Sky

Tough Mama Survival

Tough Mama Means Business

Table of Contents

Chapter 1

Yellowstone

The morning sun cast a golden hue across the Hayden Valley, painting the geysers and hot springs in shimmering shades of orange and gold. Steam rose lazily from the earth, a familiar sight in this geothermal wonderland, a constant reminder of the raw power simmering beneath Yellowstone's seemingly serene surface. Park Ranger Noah Thompson, his weathered face creased in a familiar expression of peaceful contemplation, patrolled the boardwalk, the scent of pine and sulfur heavy in the air. He'd seen countless sunrises over the park, each one a breathtaking masterpiece. Today, however, something felt different.

A subtle tremor, barely perceptible, ran through the ground. Noah paused, hand instinctively resting on the worn leather of his ranger holster. It was a fleeting sensation, easily dismissed as a minor earthquake, something not uncommon in this tectonically active region. He continued his patrol, but the feeling of unease lingered, a persistent hum beneath the tranquility of the morning. The geysers, usually erupting with predictable regularity, seemed…off. Old Faithful, typically a punctual giant, hesitated, its usual powerful expulsion delayed, the water sputtering uncertainly before finally surging skyward.

Later that morning, while observing the Biscuit and Black Sand Basins, Noah noticed other peculiarities. The usually vibrant colors of the hot springs appeared muted, the water's temperature fluctuating wildly. He checked his handheld seismograph, a routine measure, but the readings were slightly erratic. Again, he dismissed it as typical geothermal variability. He'd been a ranger in Yellowstone for over fifteen years; he knew the park's temperamental nature. But the persistent feeling of disquiet gnawed at him. He felt a shift in the very air itself—an almost imperceptible change in pressure, a subtle vibration that resonated deep within his bones.

At the Yellowstone Volcano Observatory, Dr. Madison Malone, a seismologist renowned for her meticulous observations and data analysis, stared intensely at the monitors displaying seismic data. A growing sense of alarm replaced her usual calm demeanor, and she furrowed her brow. Lines on the seismographs, normally representing the background hum of tectonic activity, were spiking with alarming frequency and intensity. The data was undeniable; it defied all established patterns. The tremors weren't merely minor quakes; they were a precursor to something far more significant, something cataclysmic.

Madison ran additional diagnostics, cross-referencing the data with historical records and geological models. The numbers spoke a terrifying language—a language of escalating pressure building within the earth's crust, a language predicting an impending super volcanic eruption. Her heart pounded in her chest as she realized the sheer magnitude of the impending disaster. The scale of potential devastation dwarfed anything she had ever encountered in her career or even imagined. Yellowstone, a place of unparalleled beauty, was on the brink of unimaginable destruction.

As the day wore on, the subtle unease morphed into a palpable sense of dread. Both intensity and frequency of the initial tremors increased, shaking the ground beneath Noah's feet. The once-serene landscape now vibrated with a menacing energy. The erratic and unsettling behavior of the animals, normally oblivious to humans, showed their agitation. Bison stampeded across the plains, their bellows echoing across the valley. Elk abandoned their usual grazing grounds, their movements frenzied and panicked. Even the normally placid deer exhibited a heightened state of anxiety, their wide eyes reflecting the growing chaos. The air grew thick with a palpable sense of fear, a primal dread that seemed to emanate from the very heart of the earth.

Now drooping and wilted, the once-vibrant wildflowers, vibrant splashes of color against the lush greenery, could no longer withstand the incessant trembling and heat. Erupting in unpredictable spasms, the geysers spouted scalding water, a change from their normally predictable power. Sediment stirred from the depths, muddied and clouded the normally crystal-clear waters of the rivers and lakes. With relentless tremors, the ground swelled and subsided, as if breathing, creating cracks and fissures. Nature's magnificent landscape, a testament to its own power, was steadily succumbing to a force beyond human comprehension. Yellowstone's beauty, once a source of wonder and awe, was quickly becoming a terrifying omen of impending doom. The very air seemed to crackle with a foreboding energy, a tangible manifestation of the immense pressure building beneath the surface.

The humming fluorescent lights overhead cast a sterile glow across the cramped lab. Madison Mallone gazed at the screen in front of her, brushing back the escaping black curly hair, the graph of seismic activity pulsating like a heartbeat. Each jagged peak sent a flutter of unease coursing through her. She had been studying this region for years, but never had she seen such alarming data.

As the day wore on, the subtle unease morphed into a palpable sense of dread. Both intensity and frequency of the initial tremors increased, shaking the ground beneath Noah's feet. The once-serene landscape now vibrated with a menacing energy. The erratic and unsettling behavior of the animals, normally oblivious to humans, showed their agitation. Bison stampeded across the plains, their bellows echoing across the valley. Elk abandoned their usual grazing grounds, their movements frenzied and panicked. Even the normally placid deer exhibited a heightened state of anxiety, their wide eyes reflecting the growing chaos. The air grew thick with a palpable sense of fear, a primal dread that seemed to emanate from the very heart of the earth.

The sheer force of the tremors overwhelmed Noah, tried to make sense of the chaos unfolding around him. He attempted to contact the park headquarters, but communication lines were already failing. The escalating frequency of the tremors was affecting the electrical infrastructure. He watched, horrified, as trees swayed violently, their branches thrashing like tormented limbs. The very landscape of Yellowstone was in turmoil, a chaotic dance of earth and fire. He knew, deep down, that this was no ordinary seismic activity. This was something far more profound, far more destructive—something that would forever alter the face of Yellowstone and, potentially, the world.

Miles away, Madison's finding were being reviewed and verified by a team of scientists. The data was irrefutable; a super volcanic eruption was imminent. The magnitude of the potential catastrophe was almost beyond comprehension. The eruption wouldn't simply be a local event; it would trigger widespread devastation, sending a massive plume of ash into the stratosphere, plunging vast swatches of the planet into darkness. The resulting climate change would wreak havoc on agriculture and weather patterns across the globe, leading to famine and societal collapse. The sheer scale of destruction was unimaginable, a nightmare scenario that threatened the very existence of civilization as they knew it.

The weight of responsibility pressed heavily on Madison's shoulders. She knew she had to act quickly, had to warn people, and had to do everything in her power to prevent a potential global catastrophe. But communicating this information, conveying the urgency and the enormity of the threat to the wider world was proving to be incredibly difficult. The situation's reality was so overwhelming it was nearly incomprehensible, much less explainable to the public and authorities. Because of the widespread devastation, humans could do little. The task felt insurmountable, a Sisyphean burden of almost unimaginable proportions. But Madison couldn't afford to falter; the lives of millions, perhaps billions, depended on her swift and effective action. The fate of the world hung precariously in the balance, and someone tasked her with issuing the warning that would decide humanity's future.

Undeniably, the situation was urgent. Noah, witnessing the unfolding chaos firsthand, and Madison, grappling with the horrifying implications of her data, knew that time was running out. Yellowstone's majestic beauty, a testament to earth's power and splendor, became the stage for a catastrophic event of unimaginable proportions. By morning, a violent, earth-shattering symphony of destruction had replaced the morning's subtle tremors. Paradise's transformation, the idyllic paradise, was about to become a scene of unprecedented devastation. Before unmatched destruction, there is calm. An unimaginable force would soon consume the serene landscape. The force would change forever the beautiful, peaceful Yellowstone they knew and loved.

The seismographs were producing a thunderous sound. Lines that had previously danced a gentle jig of tectonic activity now thrashed wildly, a frantic scribble across the screen. Adison slammed her fist on the desk, the force barely registering against the rising panic in her chest. The data was undeniable, a stark, horrifying portrait of the impending disaster. This wasn't just another earthquake swarm; this was the prelude to a super volcanic eruption of unprecedented scale. The numbers themselves were a chilling testament to the immense pressure building beneath Yellowstone's seeming placid surface. Pressure readings, normally within a predictable range, had soared to levels never recorded. The magma chamber, vast and unimaginable, was nearing its breaking point.

She stared at the thermal imaging maps, watching as areas of increased heat expanded, spreading like a malignant tumor across the park's landscape. The ground itself was changing, swelling and bulging in places, cracks snaking across the earth's surface like livid scars. GPS data showed centimeters of ground deformation per hour, a rate that sped up with every passing minute. This wasn't just a gradual shift; it was a violent heaving of the earth, a desperate struggle against the immense force trying to break free. The data wasn't just numbers on a screen; it was a death sentence, written in the language of science, precise and terrifyingly accurate.

Madison worked in a frenetic blur of activity, cross-checking data, running simulations, and attempting to refine their predictions. It was only a question of when, not if, the eruption would occur. How soon was the only remaining question? Scientists predicted a volcanic eruption of unprecedented magnitude. The ash plume alone would reach stratospheric heights, blanketing vast areas of North America in a suffocating blanket of volcanic debris. The impact on global climate would be catastrophic, triggering a volcanic winter that could last for years, possibly decades. A cascading chain of ecological disasters would follow, affecting agriculture, water resources, and the very air itself, creating conditions that would render large parts of the planet inhabitable.

"Madison! Are those figures accurate?" a voice called from behind her, pulling her from her concentration.

"Absolutely, Dr. Franklin," she replied without turning around. "The tremors have been intensifying over the last month. If the current patterns continue, we're looking at the possibility of a significant eruption."

Footsteps approached, and she could sense the skepticism emanating from the older seismologist. "You know, the government will dismiss this as a routine fluctuation. They always do. You can't expect them to take action based on predictions alone. It's only been around 700,000 years since the last eruption."

With a sigh, Madison finally turned to face her colleague. His brow furrowed, and the lines on his forehead deepened with concern; however, she knew he didn't share her conviction. "Was that you making a joke?" she laughed.

"Every scientist in the field would agree with me if they knew— if they paid attention," she argued, fighting the frustration bubbling beneath the surface. "The patterns are all there, and it's not just about the data. It's about our responsibility to act!"

Dr. Franklin rubbed his temples, shaking his head. "You've got to be careful, Madison. You sensationalize, and people will ignore you completely. Calm down; it could just be natural fluctuations."

Madison interjected, "Are you aware if you read my latest reports, the Yellowstone River has made a five percent shift toward the south? And if I say nothing, even though I believed something would happen, many people could die." Madison's jaw tightened. Natural fluctuations. Those words echoed in her mind, dredging up past warnings ignored, lives lost because of complacency. "I won't be silent. Lives are at stake. You have earthquakes, ground depression, shifting of waterways. What more do you want?"

She returned to her work, typing quickly to complete her report. The sound of shuffling papers and distant chatter faded into the background; her focus was unwavering. She needed to write an interesting report—a call to action that would be impossible to ignore.

After hours of labor, Madison leaned back in her chair, her body aching from the tension, and stared at the printed pages strewn about her desk. With a deep breath, she prepared to submit her preliminary findings to the geological board. It was the moment she had worked tirelessly towards, yet anxiety clawed at her insides.

Madison ran additional diagnostics, cross-referencing the data with historical records and geological models. The numbers spoke a terrifying language – a language of escalating pressure building within the earth's crust, a language predicting an impending super volcanic eruption. Her heart pounded in her chest as she realized the sheer magnitude of the impending disaster. The scale of potential devastation dwarfed anything she had ever encountered in her career or even imagined. Yellowstone, a place of unparalleled beauty, was on the brink of unimaginable destruction.

Simultaneously, across the park, Noah felt the earth shudder beneath his feet, a tremor far more violent than any he had experienced before. He stumbled, his grip tightening on his ranger radio. Static crackled; the communication network, already strained, was on the verge of complete failure. The air, once crisp and clean, was thick with the acrid smell of sulfur, a pungent reminder of the immense power slumbering below. Steam vents, usually emitting gentle plumes of vapor, now spewed forth powerful jets of super-heated water and steam, their roars echoing across the valley. The ground, normally solid and stable, felt soft and yielding, like walking on a giant, restless beast.

He witnessed the ground bucking and fracturing, creating gaping fissures that swallowed trees whole. Once solid and stable, the earth's surface became a fractured wasteland, a testament to cataclysmic forces. A terrifying and chaotic display of earth's raw power steadily replaced the beauty of Yellowstone. A nightmarish scene of violence and destruction now replaced the once-pristine landscape. The delicate balance of nature, maintained for millennia, was crumbling before his eyes. The majestic landscape, once a symbol of peace and tranquility, was rapidly being transformed into a scene of terrifying chaos.

Usually calm in the presence of humans, the wildlife was utterly panicked. Bison stampeded in frenzied herds, their bellows echoing the earth's tremors. Elk, normally graceful and serene, bolted in blind terror, their panicked cries adding to the cacophony. Birds, their usual melodies silenced, took flight in disoriented flocks, their wings beating a frantic rhythm against the darkening sky. Even the smaller animals, usually timid and elusive, fled in frenzied bursts of energy, driven by a primal instinct to escape the impending catastrophe. The park, usually teeming with life, was emptying, its inhabitants fleeing from the encroaching doom. It was a mass exodus driven by fear, a profound and deeply instinctive understanding of an indescribable cataclysm.

As the day wore on, the subtle unease morphed into a palpable sense of dread. The initial tremors escalated in both intensity and frequency, shaking the very ground beneath Noah's feet. The once-serene landscape now vibrated with a menacing energy. Normally oblivious to humans, the animals' erratic and unsettling behavior betrayed their agitation. Bison stampeded across the plains, their bellows echoing across the valley. Elk abandoned their usual grazing grounds, their movements frenzied and panicked. Even the normally placid deer exhibited a heightened state of anxiety, their wide eyes reflecting the growing chaos. A palpable sense of fear, a primal dread emanating from the earth's core, thickened the air.

Vibrant wildflowers, once vibrant splashes of color against lush greenery, now drooped and wilted, their delicate stems unable to withstand the incessant trembling. Fading to muted and dull hues, the radiant colors of the geysers and hot springs were disappearing. Sediment, stirred from the depths, clouded the once crystal-clear water. Relentless tremors caused the ground to breathe, swelling and subsiding, cracking the earth's surface. The beauty of

Yellowstone, once a source of wonder and awe, was rapidly transforming into a terrifying omen of impending doom. The very air seemed to crackle with a foreboding energy, a tangible manifestation of the immense pressure building beneath the surface.

Noah, overwhelmed by the sheer force of the tremors, tried to make sense of the chaos unfolding around him. Noah tried desperately to contact park headquarters, but the radio remained stubbornly silent, the static a constant, unnerving reminder of the failing infrastructure. The escalating frequency of the tremors was affecting the electrical infrastructure. He watched, horrified, as trees swayed violently, their branches thrashing like tormented limbs. The very landscape of Yellowstone was in turmoil, a chaotic dance of earth and fire. He knew, deep down, that this was no ordinary seismic activity. This was something far more profound, far more destructive – something that would forever alter the face of Yellowstone and, potentially, the world. He knew he had to escape, had to find safety, but the sheer scale of the unfolding disaster was overwhelming. The vast and incomprehensible threat was so enormous it seemed surreal. As far as the eye could see, the caldera stretched. The breathtaking beauty of Yellowstone, a place he had always cherished, was becoming a terrifying symbol of nature's raw and unstoppable power. The tranquil serenity that once defined the park was now a distant memory, replaced by the violent and chaotic dance of impending doom.

Both Noah and Madison felt the crushing weight of the impending disaster. Scientific data confirmed Noah's firsthand observation: Yellowstone's dormant super-volcano was awakening, and this awakening would be cataclysmic. A violent, unstoppable force, born from subtle morning tremors, tore at the earth's very fabric. An inferno of unimaginable proportions was about to consume the beautifully landscaped place of peace and tranquility. Yellowstone's serene beauty was being replaced by the stark reality of its impending destruction. Terror and chaos transformed the familiar landscape, terrifyingly foreshadowing the unimaginable devastation to come. The world, as they knew it, was about to end.

Chapter 2

The Lab

In her state-of-the-art lab, Madison's findings were being reviewed and verified by a team of scientists. The data was irrefutable; a super volcanic eruption was imminent. The magnitude of the potential catastrophe was almost beyond comprehension. The eruption wouldn't simply be a local event; it would trigger widespread devastation, sending a massive plume of ash into the stratosphere, plunging vast swathes of the planet into darkness. The resulting climate change would devastate global agriculture and weather patterns, causing famine and societal collapse. The sheer scale of destruction was unimaginable, a nightmare scenario that threatened the very existence of civilization as they knew it.

Madison felt the heavy weight of responsibility on her shoulders. She knew she had to be vocal, had to warn people, and had to do everything in her power to prevent a potential global catastrophe. But communicating this information, conveying the urgency and the enormity of the threat to the wider world was proving to be incredibly difficult. The situation's reality was so overwhelming it was nearly incomprehensible, much less explainable to the public and authorities. The widespread devastation made human action nearly impossible. Feeling insurmountable, the task seemed a Sisyphean burden of almost unimaginable proportions. But Madison couldn't afford to falter; the lives of millions, perhaps billions, depended on her swift and effective action. The world's fate hung precariously in the balance, and she received issuing the warning that would decide humanity's future.

As the clock ticked closer to six, she gathered her things, determined to hand-deliver her report and advocate for urgency. Stepping out of the lab, the murmur of students met her discussing their weekend plans. For them, life continued—unbothered by the silent threat brewing beneath the earth.

Madison reached her car, the evening air sharp against her skin. She tossed her bag in the passenger seat and took a moment to inhale deeply, trying to quell the storm of worry brewing inside her. Outside, the sunset painted the sky in hues of orange and violet. But all she could think of was the ground beneath her—and how it could rupture, consuming everything she loved.

Determined, she drove towards the geological board, her mind racing. Would they listen? Would there be time to prepare?

The urgency of the situation was undeniable. Noah, witnessing the unfolding chaos firsthand, and Madison, grappling with the horrifying implications of her data, knew that time was running out. Yellowstone's majestic beauty, a testament to the earth's power and splendor, became the stage for a catastrophic event of unimaginable proportions. What began as subtle tremors of the morning had transformed into a violent, earth-shattering symphony of destruction. Unprecedented devastation was about to transform the idyllic paradise. The serene landscape was soon to be consumed by a force far greater than anything they could imagine. An unimaginable force would forever change the Yellowstone everyone knew and loved.

Halfway to her destination, her phone buzzed on the dashboard. Glancing at the caller ID, she saw Noah Thompson's name. A familiar warmth surged in her chest as she answered, the images of her day vanishing momentarily. She met Noah at Yellowstone two months ago while she was checking on the seismic monitors. Since then, they always find a reason to talk. Earthquakes, lava, eruptions. Typical topics for a couple just dating.

Madison's love life has been nothing to take to the bank. Non-existent is the better descriptor. Even growing up, it was hard to relate to the opposite sex, but Noah was different. He loved nature.

He was the perfect park ranger. Just hearing his name alone gave her butterflies in her stomach.

"Hey, the sun is setting. Why don't you take a break after this? Meet me by the old lodge? With all this shaking going on, I want to make sure everything is okay there."

"Really? At the lodge?" The lodge is a big log cabin with a stone fireplace. Interesting part of the lodge is all taxidermized animals: a bear, and various birds, strategically placed. The main room was warm and cozy. Noah had thick carpets on the wood floor. The worn leather felt like soft butter. What made the room perfect were the handmade quilts his grandmother would send him. The lodge was near the edge of Delusion Lake and on a sunny day, the dancing light of the lake would bounce off the glass on the windows. Going up to the lodge would give her the chance to check on the lake to see if the quakes have caused any changes.

"Trust me," he urged, and she could hear the playful grin in his voice.

"Okay, fine. Just for a little while," she relented, the thought of unwinding with Noah already lightening her mood.

After hanging up, Madison put the report submission on hold for just a moment longer. A brief respite wouldn't hurt. Steering her car towards the old lodge felt like a minor act of rebellion against the weight of the world. The thought of Noah made her smile. "He would make one lucky woman happy," she whispered.

As she arrived, the landscape transformed into serene pines and wildflowers, an oasis against the backdrop of her chaotic thoughts. Noah was standing outside, his silhouette framed by the dim light of the fading sun. He turned at the sound of her car, a genuine smile spreading across his face as he approached her. Madison was driving him crazy! She did not know how beautiful she was and had the biggest loving heart he's ever seen. Noah has been unlucky in love his entire life. Being a park ranger was not an exciting prospect for what a woman would want. Truth be told, Noah connected better with foxes and bears than women.

"Hey there! Just in time," he said, his enthusiasm infectious. Noah had a way of making everything feel lighter, like the sun breaking through heavy clouds.

"Am I really? I almost turned around and went straight to the board to submit the report," Madison admitted, stepping out of the car and inhaling the fresh scent of pine mingled with the cool evening air.

"You're here now, and that's what matters," he replied, gently taking her bag from her shoulder and setting it aside. The smell of the sulfur was overpowering, and the wildflowers were sagging and dying.

"This is amazing," Madison marveled, her heart swelling with appreciation. "You really went all out!"

Something was wrong, but Madison couldn't put her finger on it.

"Noah! Look!" She was looking towards the lake. "Stop the car!"

She took a deep breath, capturing the essence of the moment before sharing her fears. The short walk to the lake showed that most of the lake had disappeared. There was a small portion of the lake left, but the steam and bubbling fumaroles were all that remained of the site they were at. The bubbling mud was everywhere! All the steam showed that the temperature must have been over 212 degrees. "Noah, the temperature of this area is from 100 to 1800 degrees Fahrenheit! An entire lake just bubbled off! I have to get back to the center! "The eruption! The seismic activity is ramping up more than ever. I fear we might not be prepared— people won't see it coming. The odds are so against what I'm thinking, but a big red flag is waving. They will blame me if I remain silent.

Madison nodded and attempted to reach Dr. Franklin. She's left so many messages and she couldn't reach him.

But as the night deepened, and the stars painted the sky, a distant rumble echoed from deep within the earth. Madison paused mid-sentence, her mind racing back to her work. In an instant, everything shifted in her awareness.

"Did you hear that?" she asked, her heart racing.

Noah narrowed his gaze, tilting his head to listen. "It must be thunder rolling in from the west. We might want to head inside soon if it does."

"No. It's not thunder." The dread crept back into her veins as she thought of the data she had seen earlier. "This... this feels different. I think its seismic activity."

"What do you mean?"

"I've studied enough to know the difference. It's not just the wind or some storm; it's something deeper." She pulled out her phone, heart pounding as she opened a seismology app she often used.

Her heart sank as she saw the alerts buzzing in. Multiple tremors had just registered. The readings were unlike anything she had encountered before. The seismographs screamed. Lines that had previously danced a gentle jig of tectonic activity now thrashed wildly, a frantic scribble across the screen. Madison slammed her fist on the desk, the force barely registering against the rising panic in her chest. The data was undeniable, a stark, horrifying portrait of the impending disaster. This wasn't just another earthquake swarm; this was the prelude to a super volcanic eruption of unprecedented scale. The numbers themselves were a chilling testament to the immense pressure building beneath Yellowstone's seemingly placid surface. Pressure readings, normally within a predictable range, had soared to levels never recorded. The magma chamber, vast and unimaginable, was nearing its breaking point. This was no harmless swarm.

She stared at the thermal imaging maps, watching as areas of increased heat expanded, spreading like a malignant tumor across the park's landscape. The ground itself was changing, swelling and bulging in places, cracks snaking across the earth's surface like livid scars. GPS data showed centimeters of ground deformation per hour, a rate that accelerated with every passing minute. This wasn't just a gradual shift; it was a violent heaving of the earth, a desperate struggle against the immense force trying to break free. The data wasn't just numbers on a screen; it was a death sentence, written in the language of science, precise and terrifyingly accurate.

"Noah, we need to go. Something is happening at Yellowstone. I can't ignore this. We have to warn people!" she urged, grabbing her bag and instinctively looking towards the direction of the park, as if she could sense the impending catastrophe looming over it.

Madison worked in a frenetic blur of activity, cross-checking data, running simulations, and attempting to refine their predictions. It was not a question of if the eruption would occur, but when. How soon was the only remaining question. In human history, no other eruption even came close to the predicted one's magnitude and scale. The ash plume alone would reach stratospheric heights, blanketing vast areas of North America in a suffocating blanket of volcanic debris. The impact on global climate would be catastrophic, triggering a volcanic winter that could last for years, possibly decades. A cascading chain of ecological disasters would follow, affecting agriculture, water resources, and the very air itself, creating conditions that would render large parts of the planet uninhabitable.

Noah looked concerned, but he quickly stood, capturing her shoulders with steady hands. "Okay, let's figure this out, but we can't start panicking now. We need a plan. What do you want to do?"

Madison could feel panic rising in her throat, but she forced herself to breathed steadily. "First, we need to reach the geological board. If they won't listen, then we go public. We can't let this slip through the cracks."

"Let's do it."

As they hurried back to the car, Madison felt the weight of the world settling heavily on her shoulders again. But in that moment, she also felt something else: resolve. She would fight for every life, starting with the people she loved.

"Madison?" Noah's voice broke through her thoughts as he started the engine.

"Yeah?"

"I'm with you. Whatever happens, we'll face it together."

A smile tugged at the corners of Madison's lips despite the turmoil raging within her. It was a promise, a tether to something solid amidst the uncertainty. "Thank you, Noah. I need that right now. We need to be prepared because we are out of here. Fill the car up with food, water, and medical supplies. I'm going to make sure we can get as many people as possible to leave."

With the road stretching out before them, Lake Yellowstone's flickering reflections danced in the moonlight. The weight of impending disaster lingered in the air, but the warmth of Noah's presence made it a bit more bearable.

As they drove, Madison's mind raced with calculations and the potential implications of the seismic readings. The potential for a catastrophic eruption felt so real. Could she really get them to listen? The thought solidified her determination.

They arrived at the geological board's office just as the building's lights flickered ominously in the twilight. Madison jumped out of the car, her heels clicking against the pavement as she rushed towards the entrance, Noah close behind.

The board—an austere collection of offices filled with scientists and bureaucrats—was underwhelming in its appearance, yet it held the power to make crucial decisions that could affect countless lives. Inside, the sudden hum of activity struck her as both reassuring and frustrating; everyone was fixated on screens, oblivious to the impending threats outside.

"Madison!" called a familiar voice as Dr. Franklin emerged, eyes wide. She crossed the room, urgency thrumming in her veins. "I assume you've got something major to discuss?"

"Please, it's urgent! We need to assess the seismic reports! The data from tonight shows significant activity that could lead to an eruption!" Madison's voice was steady, but her heart raced as she scanned the room for the faces she knew would be skeptical. "Delusion Lake has disappeared, replaced by fumaroles!"

Dr. Franklin glanced at her feverishly before shaking his head. "We just held a meeting. The committee decided that the recent tremors are not unusual—"

"Not unusual? Does anyone but me know about Delusion Lake?" Madison interrupted, unable to contain her frustration. "These aren't just minor fluctuations! Dr. Franklin, listen to the data trends over the last month! If we don't act now, there could be irreversible consequences! We are missing one of the largest lakes in the park, the Yellowstone River has shifted, and we have magma moving under our feet!"

Noah stood close by, offering silent support, but she could see the tension in Dr. Franklin's shoulders. The seismologist's eyes softened for a moment, caught in the passionate intensity of her words—but doubt still clouded them.

"Madison, I understand your concern, but we can't jump to conclusions—"

"In this field, data builds conclusions!" All we need is a full analysis, and you'll see I'm not exaggerating! Please look!" she pressed, desperation spilling into her words. "These changes tick every box!"

A faint murmur of interest began weaving through the gathered scientists, and Madison seized the moment, quickly navigating towards the nearest desk. "Look at this!" she exclaimed, pulling up her report on the shared monitor. The screen showcased seismic graphs depicting the dramatic rise in activity leading up to the eruption.

A few in the room began leaning in, their interest piqued. Madison took a deep breath, encouraged by the reactions, and continued, "You can see the spikes—not just isolated incidents, but a clear and expressive trend. We have a duty to protect the citizens and the tourists, and this place is no longer safe!"

Dr. Franklin crossed his arms, his expression still skeptical, but others started whispering among themselves, evaluating the data she presented.

"There's a risk of exponential escalation," she added urgently. "We need to prepare evacuation protocols for the surrounding communities immediately! Anything less would be a disservice to our responsibility as scientists."

A tall man with silvering hair and a badge reading "Board Chair" stepped forward. He had a presence that commanded attention, and Madison's heart raced as he approached. "Dr. Mallone, can you vouch for the reliability of this data? We need definitive assurance before we raise the alarm."

"I've dedicated my career to understanding the volcanic systems of Yellowstone. I wouldn't be here advocating if I wasn't certain," she replied earnestly, meeting his gaze. "We can't afford complacency. Tourists, residents, everyone, needs to get out! Now!"

The board chair nodded, his expression contemplative. "Dr. Franklin, we may need to rerun the model data and see your recommendations for a preliminary assessment."

Madison's heart lifted, hope igniting within her. "Thank you. I know you won't regret this."

Just then, a loud rumble echoed through the building, shaking the walls and causing papers to flutter like leaves in a gust. Gasps rang out, and Madison's stomach dropped.

"Was that an earthquake?" one scientist asked, fear creeping into their tones.

"Yes," she replied, her thumping pulse echoing the seismic activity beneath their feet. "We're already feeling the effects. We have magma flowing under our feet!"

"Everyone, back to your stations!" the board chair commanded, and immediate chaos erupted as people began scrambling to monitor the activity.

"Noah!" Madison called, her heart racing as instinct pushed her to find him amidst the commotion. She spotted him near the entrance, his expression a mix of concern and resolve.

"Did you feel that?" he asked, urgency in his tone. "Yes, and it's exactly what I was afraid of," Madison replied, her voice steady despite the surrounding turmoil. "The time for more research is past. I'm going to get the word out. I can only hope I get fired if I'm wrong. Noah, please, get everyone out of here! Tell everyone!"

Noah nodded; his gaze sharp with focus. "Let's keep the momentum going, then. I'll make sure they know what's happening at the park. You keep on them here."

Madison felt a surge of gratitude, but also a flicker of anxiety at the thought of the unknown. "Be careful, okay?"

He smiled slightly, a reassured glint in his eyes. "I'm used to danger. Save your energy for your fight here."

As Noah slipped away to head toward the communications room, Madison returned her focus to the board members, who were already pulling together their resources to address the seismic event. The atmosphere bustled with urgency, and she sensed that her earlier attempts to alert them were paying off.

"Dr. Mallone, we're rerunning the models now," Dr. Franklin announced, his tone more cooperative than before. "We'll need your input on what parameters to focus on."

Madison moved to the boardroom table, where several displays flickered with seismic readings. The graphs danced before her eyes, the bright colors highlighting the tremors rocketing through the region. "Change the scale to reflect the last month's data and compare it with historical events. We need to contextualize the spikes against previous eruptions." In the meantime, Madison was packing all of her research, her laptop, and other essential monitoring equipment.

As they worked, the board members crowded around her, some scrutinizing data, others calling in local emergency services for assessments. The intensity of the moment battered against Madison, but she stood firm, her resolve coalescing into focus.

Minutes felt like hours as the seismic activity intensified. Madison could feel the building tremble beneath her feet, and she glanced toward the windows to see the trees outside swaying violently in the increasingly tumultuous winds.

A voice called from the entryway. "We're getting reports of evacuations starting from the park perimeter!" It was one of the geological staff members, urgency etched across her features.

"Good, but it's not enough," Madison said, turning back to the board. "We need a wider alert. Emergency services must mobilize not just for residents but for all tourists and workers in the area."

"Agreed," the board chair said, his brow furrowed in concentration. "Let's draft a public announcement and advise immediate evacuation plans for those in the surrounding zones."

Madison could barely suppress the swell of emotions—relief, fear, and urgency swirling within her—but didn't allow herself to relented. "We also need to prepare for options of shelter beyond the immediate vicinity, in case of mass evacuations."

Time passed in a blur of technical discussions and logistical planning. As they worked, the rumbling outside intensified, shakes rippling through the building at increasingly frequent intervals.

Finally, after what felt like a grueling marathon, one scientist halted the ongoing discussion. "The seismic patterns are now broadcasting a distinct signal showing rising pressure. This could be it."

Madison's stomach knotted as she looked around the room. The fear on everyone's face mirrored her own apprehension. "Then we need to escalate our efforts. Whatever happens, we need to be ready to assist those who might not evacuate in time. When Yellowstone blows, we are looking at a minimum of 15 feet of ash! People will die! Everyone needs to get as far away as possible now!"

Just as those words left her mouth, another powerful tremor rocked the building. Papers flew from the tables, and the lights flickered violently.

"Everyone take cover!" the board chair shouted, and Madison instinctively ducked under the table, shielding her head with her arms.

"Are you okay?" Madison heard Noah's voice nearby, and she forced herself to peek out from under the table to see him crouched low, his expression a mixture of concern and determination.

"Just stay close," she said, her heart pounding against her ribcage.

The tremor subsided, but a thick silence settled over the room. Fear crackled in the air like electricity, and she could see the uncertainty mirrored in the eyes surrounding her.

After a moment, the board chair emerged from under his own makeshift shelter, directing them to exit the room. "We need to move to a safer area. Follow my lead."

Madison exchanged a glance with Noah. He took her hand and squeezed it tightly, an anchor amidst the chaos. "We are making the evacuation orders and taking everyone out!"

They filed out into the hall, making their way toward the exit. Outside, chaos reigned as personnel scrambled to secure data and communicate with emergency responders. The ground trembled intermittently beneath them, dust falling from the ceiling.

"We won't get everyone out in time," Madison stated, her voice low but heavy with dread. "People need to know what's happening."

Noah leaned close to her, the intensity in his eyes. "Then we have to take the message to them. If the board won't send alerts fast enough, we have to do it ourselves."

"Are you suggesting we go to the park?" Madison's heart raced. "No," Noah said with a determined shake of his head.

"Not just the park. We need to get to the surrounding communities—Jackson, Cody—places that could be in the path of ash fallout or affected by tremors. They need to evacuate, and fast. Call the police and let them know to evacuate immediately. We should get some buses from the school and load up whoever needs help or doesn't have transportation. Place a call to FEMA as well. Our secret will be out soon!"

Madison felt her heart racing with adrenaline, a mix of fear and excitement coursing through her veins. "You're right. We can't wait for bureaucratic decisions; we have to be the messengers."

As they moved with purpose through the chaos of the building, deciding on their primary objectives was vital. Madison spotted one of the staff members hurriedly inputting information into a report. "You!" she shouted, rushing over. "We need a list of numbers for the emergency contacts of nearby towns. We need to relay the risks immediately!"

"Yes, ma'am," the young woman replied, her fingers flying across the keyboard.

Noah and Madison exchanged encouraging glances, their determination radiating off each other like a charge. Madison felt emboldened as they worked, growing into their roles as protectors of their community.

Less than a minute later, the staff member turned back, a list in hand. "Here you go. It's not complete, but it's a start. Do you want me to call them?"

"No time!" Madison instructed. "We need to mobilize ourselves. Noah, can you grab a car—the truck outside? We'll need to cover more ground. I need a warning to go out to the residents that I will have buses in front of the schools. We welcome anyone who needs transportation. Fill up the school buses. Load everyone up and let's get the hell off this mountain!"

"On it," he said quickly, leaving her side and heading towards the nearest exit.

With a mixture of nerves and excitement, Madison continued working with the staff member. "Have you heard if any media outlets are here? We need to get in touch with them to spread the word even faster."

"I think there's a local news crew outside covering the earthquake reports," she confirmed. "I can help you get there."

"Great! Let's go!"

Chapter 3

Volcano

They vacated the building, stepping out into the frigid night air. Outside, the panic was palpable—a scene filled with flashing lights from emergency vehicles and people rushing about, their faces reflecting the stark reality of what was unfolding around them.

Madison spotted Noah, who had successfully commandeered a large, rugged truck embossed with the park's logo. He was already waving her over, ready for action.

As they dashed toward him, the ground rumbled again, slightly less intense but enough to provoke murmurs of fear from those nearby. "Get in!" Noah called, unlocking the doors and gesturing for them to hurry.

Madison climbed into the passenger seat, quickly relaying instructions to the staff member who had joined them. "Can you navigate to those emergency contacts while we drive to the news crew?"

"Yes—just tell me where!" she replied, breathless.

"Head towards the park entrance and take the main road to Jackson!" Madison answered, her pulse thrumming. "We'll need to make sure they get the information out fast."

Noah started the engine, and they peeled away from the unfolding chaos of the geological board. Madison felt a rush of exhilaration blend with nerves as they sped into the night, the headlights illuminating the winding roads ahead.

"Can you contact emergency services and let them know we're headed to warn the local towns?" she urged, watching as the landscape blurred around them, trees whipping by in a darkened rush.

"Already on it!" the staff member nodded, pulling out her phone and tapping the screen furiously.

Madison turned to Noah as he navigated the vehicle through the dark terrain. "You're incredible. I don't know what I'd do without you."

They continued driving, the air thick with tension as they embraced their roles with urgency. The enormity of the task ahead loomed, but the fire in Madison's heart burned brighter than ever. She couldn't shake the feeling that every decision they made now would determine the fate of countless people.

As they approached the outskirts of Jackson, news vans appeared, their bright lights illuminating the night. Madison took a deep breath, adrenaline pumping through her veins. "This is it. Let's make sure they have the information they need."

When they reached the news crews, chaos mingled with urgency. They parked the truck and hopped out, quickly identifying a reporter interviewing people on camera. Madison felt a mixture of nerves and determination swelling within her as they approached.

use me!" she called, her voice cutting through the background noise. "We need to get critical information out right now!"

The reporter turned, surprise flickering across her face. "What's going on?"

"There's been severe seismic activity at Yellowstone, triggering an imminent threat to surrounding communities," Madison explained, urgency thrumming beneath her words. "You must tell everyone to evacuate immediately!" There have also been landslides, so people need to be extra cautious while driving."

The reporter's demeanor shifted. "Can you verify that information? We need solid details for the broadcast."

"Absolutely," Madison replied, her heart racing like the blood pounding in her ears. "I'm Dr. Madison Mallone, a seismologist with Yellowstone. We observed unprecedented seismic activity tonight—tremors that suggest an imminent threat of volcanic eruption. We've seen two landslides and one of those landslides was at an evacuation site."

The news crew's attention sharpened, and the reporter quickly gestured for her cameraman to film. "We're live now," she said, pointing the camera at Madison. "Dr. Mallone, can you explain to the viewers what they should expect?"

Madison took a deep breath, focusing on the camera lens and the people who would watch, perhaps unaware of the danger closing in. "Residents of Jackson and the surrounding areas should prepare for evacuation immediately. We are getting substantial readings from Yellowstone that show an increased likelihood of eruption within the next few days. If you are able, bring food, water, and your medications. We've lost a resident when he fell into a fault with lava running through it. Stay away from fault lines and compressed ground areas."

The reporter nodded; her expression was serious. "What should people do? What are the signs they should know?"

"Everyone needs to stay alert for any changes in their environment. Sudden tremors, increased ash fall, or unusual gas and steam from the ground or water sources can signal danger," Madison explained, her science-filled mind racing. "The best course of action is to move away from the national park and head to higher ground, as well as follows local emergency guidelines. Collect all the food, water, and medications as possible. Once the ash falls, there will be no going outside. Breathing in ash will kill you as it sticks to the inside of your lungs. Also, don't wait until the last minute to leave. The ash will clog your engine and your car will stop working. Get as far away from Yellowstone as possible! Seek shelter in a cave, a basement, or anywhere the ash won't reach you. The ash gets hotter as you get closer to Yellowstone."

"Thank you, Dr. Mallone. We need everyone to heed this warning seriously. Stay tuned for more updates as we continue to monitor this developing situation," the reporter said, her voice steady.

As the segment ended, Madison felt an overwhelming surge of relief—her message was out. But it was just the beginning.

"Let's keep moving," she said to Noah and the staff member, turning to head back toward the truck. "We need to reach Cody next—those people can't wait for another moment."

"Got it. I've already begun contacting them via walkie-talkie; I'll keep updating them on time-sensitive developments," the staff member reported, her face alight with determination as they jogged back to the truck.

"So far, so good," Noah added, his voice brimming with calm. "We have some momentum now. Let's keep it going."

Climbing back into the vehicle, Madison took a moment to steady herself. "This is intense," she admitted, her hands trembling slightly as she gripped the dashboard.

"Intense but necessary," Noah replied, starting up the engine and steering them back onto the road. "If we can save just one life by getting this information out there, then it's worth the chaos."

As they drove towards Cody, the weight of their responsibility pressed down on them, heavy and urgent. Madison replayed each detail in her mind, making sure every piece of information was right. She knew mistakes could cost lives.

"Are we going to reach Cody before dawn?" the staff member asked, glancing at her watch as they navigated the winding roads through the dark.

"Yeah, if the roads stay clear and we keep this pace," Noah replied confidently. "Just stay focused on the task at hand—stay sharp, everyone."

They continued, clips of news updates from various stations filling the airwaves as they drove, warning communities of the potential danger. Madison's heart raced as she listened, grateful to see more and more people tuning in and taking the situation seriously.

Finally, as they approached Cody, the first light of dawn broke across the horizon, casting a pale glow through the trees lining the road. Madison felt renewed urgency; the townspeople's mobilization, with their headlights appearing as they moved to higher ground, encouraged them.

Noah pulled the truck over to a local emergency services command center. "This is it, Madison. Let's get them the information they need to make a proper assessment and coordinate evacuations."

Madison nodded, adrenaline surging through her. They jumped out of the truck and sprinted toward the command trailer, where officials were busy planning logistics and disseminating information.

An officer stepped outside as they approached, a frown etched across his face. "Can I help you?"

"Yes," Madison said, urgency fueling her voice. "I'm Dr. Madison Mallone from the geological board. We need to discuss immediate evacuation procedures for the area surrounding Yellowstone, based on increasing seismic activity."

"Dr. Mallone? I've seen your reports," he replied, recognition flickering in his eyes. "We have little time. What are the current figures?"

"No time for details—we need to inform all residents and prepare them to evacuate now. Gather everyone here, and I can give a briefing, but we need action immediately."

The officer quickly nodded, rallying his team as they facilitated announcements over their radios. Madison felt a surge of determination swell within her as she watched the townsfolk come together in response—all hands-on deck, ready to take action.

As the sun rose, painting the sky in vibrant pinks and golds, Madison stood before the hastily gathered crowd of local officials and residents in front of the command center. The atmosphere buzzed with tension, and she took a deep breath, steeling herself for what lay ahead.

"Thank you all for coming on such short notice," she began, her voice steady despite the whirlwind of emotions coursing through her. "As you may have heard, we are facing an unprecedented situation concerning the Yellowstone super volcano. The seismic activity we are experiencing is not just a minor anomaly; it shows a significant risk of eruption. The question is, will we contain the eruption, or will the caldera erupt?

Murmurs rippled through the crowd. Faces reflected a mix of disbelief, concern, and urgency. She caught sight of the townspeople exchanging worried glances, fear clear in their eyes.

"I know this sounds alarming," she pressed on, raising her voice slightly to command attention. "But panic won't help us. What we need is a coordinated response, effective communication, and immediate action. We must evacuate the surrounding communities—Cody, Jackson, and anyone else who might be affected."

The officer who had met them earlier stepped forward, a determined glint in his eye. "What are the signs we should watch for? How do we know when it's time to leave?"

Madison glanced at the crowd, taking in the anxious faces. "We should all be prepared for sudden tremors—like the ones we've felt tonight—and increased ashfall. The smoke from a potential eruption could block out sunlight, and hazardous gases, such as sulfur, could seep from fissures in the earth. It's essential that if you notice changes or feel strong tremors, evacuate immediately. The problem is humanity wasn't here when the last few eruptions happened. Each volcano has its own personality and we don't know Yellowstone's personality. The time to get off this mountain is now!"

The officer nodded, speaking into his radio to convey the urgency of the situation to his team. "Get me in touch with the local media. We need to broadcast this evacuation order immediately."

Madison felt a wave of relief wash over her as she watched action unfold, people beginning to spread out and organize transport for the vulnerable—elderly citizens, families with young children, anyone who might have difficulty evacuating.

"Please," she implored as everyone dispersed, "monitor your neighbors. Not everyone will hear the news quickly enough. We need to band together for safety."

"We will take care of our own!" shouted a woman from the back of the crowd, her voice ringing with resolve. "You have our backs, and we have each other."

Cheers erupted among the crowd, a powerful wave of solidarity washing over them. Encouraged, Madison felt a rush of hope igniting amidst the fear.

After a moment of regrouping, a news van arrived, its crew jumping out and ready to film. The reporter approached Madison once again, microphone in hand, brows furrowed, but eyes filled with determination. "Dr. Mallone, may I have a moment? Can you explain what specific actions residents need to take now?"

Madison turned to the camera, her heart racing as she spoke. "Yes. Community members must evacuate immediately and follow the directions given by local authorities. If you are within a fifty-mile radius of Yellowstone, please leave your homes and get as far away from the mountain as possible. Get off the mountain and avoid rivers. Stay out of the air flow. The air flow will carry the ash. This situation is developing, and we don't know how rapidly it will escalate."

"Is there a timeline? How long do we have?" The reporter pressed.

"We cannot predict the timeline exactly," Madison confessed, her heart heavy with uncertainty. "The danger is present and very real. People must act quickly. This is an intervention to avoid disaster. There are so many things that could go wrong. You must take shelter as soon as you encounter ash. It will clog the motor of your vehicle. Inhaling it will be like breathing crushed glass. It gets into the deepest passages of your lungs. I would expect to see over 15 feet of ash. Once it encounters moisture, it becomes like cement. The ash increases in temperature the closer to Yellowstone."

As the news crew continued to film, she felt a surge of urgency and adrenaline—this was just as much about saving lives as it was about ensuring her predictions didn't fall on deaf ears.

When the interview concluded, she saw Noah near the truck, speaking to a group of local emergency responders who planned evacuation routes. He caught Madison's eye and flashed her an encouraging smile.

"We have them mobilizing," he said, walking back toward her. "They're coordinating buses and informing the schools to prepare for sheltering. We're making progress."

Madison sighed, a mix of hope and exhaustion flooding her system. "It's not enough to just evacuate; we have to ensure everyone understands the risks involved."

"Agreed," Noah replied, running a hand through his hair, which was tousled from the chaos. "But this is an incredible start. You did great with the news!"

"Thanks," she said, warmth flooding her chest at his praise. "But I can't help thinking about those who aren't hearing this message as quickly as we'd like. Every second counts. This very well may be the first eruption in 700,000 years. If it's more than an eruption, the entire country will be affected and a nuclear winter. Ash will cover from sea to shining sea, eventually spreading around the world. This will cause a nuclear winter. They stood shoulder to shoulder for a moment, both taking in the surrounding scene. Emergency workers were directing traffic, while families packed bags and loaded their vehicles, visibly shaken but determined to respond to the danger. The collective spirit of the community reinforced her belief in the importance of acting quickly.

"Let's spread the word further," Noah suggested, his voice firm. "If we can reach out to other communities nearby—like Powell, for instance—we might get ahead of this. Every connection counts."

"Good idea," Madison replied, her mind racing as she thought about how they could leverage everything they'd coordinated so far. "If we can mobilize a few volunteers to spread the word, we might reach people in even those smaller towns."

Noah nodded; his expression was resolute. "Let me grab the emergency services officer I spoke to earlier. He'll have contacts we can use to set this up quicker."

While Noah ran to gather the officer, Madison walked back to the crowd that was forming, determined to maintain the momentum they'd built. She could see groups of locals conferring with one another, discussing evacuation strategies.

She approached a couple who were preparing a car. "Excuse me! Do you have a moment?"

The older man looked up; his expression was weary but resolute. "Yes, ma'am. We're just getting our things together."

"I need you to help me relay a message. We're urging everyone to check in on their neighbors, especially anyone who might be elderly or disabled. It's important that no one gets left behind," Madison said, her urgency palpable.

"Absolutely, we were just talking about that," the woman beside him replied. "We have an elderly neighbor who doesn't have any family nearby. We can offer to help her. What else can we do?"

"Spread the word as much as possible; if you can set up a small gathering in your neighborhood to ensure everyone knows what's happening, that would be incredible. We need to ensure nobody misses the evacuation order," Madison said, her voice steady. "If possible, bring food, water, and medical supplies or medication."

The couple exchanged determined glances. "We can do that. We'll start knocking on doors and get everyone prepared."

"Thank you! Every action matters right now," Madison said, a surge of gratitude flashing through her.

As she moved back toward the command center, she spotted Noah returning, this time accompanied by the emergency services officer.

"They're setting up a rapid response team to reach neighboring areas," the officer said, a sense of urgency in his voice. "We'll have people relaying the message into Powell and areas further out."

"We also need flyers or digital alerts to create awareness," Madison added quickly. "We should use social media too—get the message out through online platforms to reach as many people as possible."

The officer nodded with conviction. "I can coordinate with the town's volunteer network to spread the word quickly via social media, and we can have some flyers printed in a few minutes."

"Perfect!" Madison said, energized. "We should also connect with any other local news sources. The more people know about this, the better the response."

Chapter 4

Craggy Peak

As she discussed the strategies with Noah and the officer, they allocated specific tasks: who would handle the social media announcements, who would liaise with the volunteer networks, and who would coordinate the media updates?

Madison could feel the energy in the air shifting. The helplessness that had gripped her earlier was fading, replaced by a collective resolve.

Finally, after all the crucial discussions, a solid plan of action began taking shape. Madison felt a sense of purpose ignite within her. "Okay, everyone, let's move fast. The sooner we can get this information out there, the more lives we can save."

Noah shot her a glance filled with admiration as she rallied the group. "You're a force of nature, Madison. Let's do this."

With a resounding chorus of affirmations, they began dispersing into smaller teams, ready to take action. Madison watched as the emergency services officer issued instructions, and teams moved out, headed for different communities.

As they turned to start their rounds, Madison felt her phone vibrate. Pulling it out, she saw several missed calls from her colleagues at the geological board. With a frown, she dialed them back.

"Dr. Mallone!" came a frantic voice on the other end. "We've been receiving intense reports from the monitoring stations—we have to analyze the data in real time; it's increasing by the second. We're seeing activity at historically unprecedented levels!"

Her heart raced, dread curling in her stomach. "I'm in Cody, and we're trying to reach out to surrounding communities to ensure everyone evacuates. What are the latest readings?"

"Multiple sensors are detecting escalating ground deformation—this can lead to a significant eruption. We need to plan an emergency plan now! This is a matter of hours, potentially even less!"

Madison's breath caught in her throat. "I understand. I'll relay the urgency to the residents here and make sure we strengthen evacuation efforts! Earlier, we lost one of our residents when he fell into a collapsed fault that had lava flowing through it."

"Not good. Keep us updated, and we'll do the same from our end," the voice said before hanging up.

Madison turned to Noah; her eyes were wide with renewed intensity. "We need to double down on our efforts. The seismic activity is speeding up, and it could erupt imminently. We can't let people linger in doubt or fear!"

"No hesitation," Noah replied, his expression fierce. "Let's get moving. We'll make sure they know the urgency."

Madison quickly joined him as they made their way back to the crowd gathered near the command center. The atmosphere felt charged with purpose, and she felt solidarity stirring around her.

"Everyone!" Madison called out, her voice cutting through the chatter. "I just received crucial updates from the geological board. The seismic activity is speeding up, and the threat level has increased significantly. We're facing what could be a major eruption, and we need to act swiftly."

Gasps rippled through the crowd, faces turning pale with fear, but she pressed on, unwilling to let panic take hold. "I know this is frightening, but we must stay focused. We need to mobilize every resource available and ensure that every person in our community understands the seriousness of the situation."

A woman stepped forward, her voice trembling slightly. "What should we do? Are we in immediate danger?"

Madison nodded gravely. "Yes, we are. I cannot stress enough how important it is that we evacuate to lower ground, as far away from the mountain as possible. Please gather your essentials and do not delay. Every moment is crucial. We want to ensure that everyone gets to safety."

Noah stepped forward as well, his commanding presence bolstering her words. "If you know anyone who needs help, don't hesitate. We're requesting that everyone check on their neighbors. We're a community, and we need to come together."

The urgency in their voices galvanized the crowd. People began moving more quickly, loading vehicles with belongings, gathering family members, and reaching out to neighbors.

"What about the schools?" a concerned father asked. "What should we do about the children?"

"Right now, I suggest contacting the schools to inform them of the evacuation protocol. The emergency services are working on shelter arrangements and should be in touch with school officials soon," Madison replied. "If you have children, please prioritize picking them up immediately and heading off this mountain. We don't know the extent of the eruption, but I suggest planning for the worst. This is a super volcano, not a geyser."

A sense of clarity emerged amidst the rising tension, and Madison felt empowered as she assisted wherever she could— leading discussions with families, helping coordinate transport for those who couldn't drive themselves, and fielding questions.

As the sun fully rose, the day illuminated the chaos unfolding, a stark contrast to the determined spirit of the community. With a few volunteers, Madison began knocking on doors to alert anyone who hadn't yet heard.

"Let's start with this block," she said, turning to a group of locals gathered near the command center. "We'll split up and cover more ground. Be respectful but direct—people need to know they can't hesitate."

As they moved through the streets, knocking on doors and calling out for anyone inside, Madison felt a sense of unity with each person who joined their efforts. She remembered the essence of community—the support, the commitment to look out for one another.

After several houses, Madison's heart sank momentarily when she knocked on the door of an elderly couple who weren't home.

"Maybe they're out getting supplies?" one volunteer said, but Madison felt a nagging worry.

"Let's look for a neighbor who might know," she suggested. "We can't leave anyone behind."

The group reconsidered and asked surrounding neighbors if they had seen the couple. They were lucky enough to find a neighbor who had seen them just a few hours ago, reassuring them they were likely at the local market.

Continuing their rounds, they found a few more families that needed help packing their belongings. Madison felt satisfaction in knowing she was making a difference, but dread still lurked in the back of her mind—what if they couldn't reach everyone?

Once they finished their neighborhood checks, the small volunteer team regrouped at the command center. "What's the latest?" Madison asked as she fell into step beside Noah.

"Evacuation sites are being set up at the high school and community center, and emergency services have shuttled people who don't have transportation," he answered, relief clear in his eyes. "They're prepared for shelters, and more buses are arriving."

Just then, Madison's phone buzzed again. She glanced at the screen—another call from the geological board. With a knot tightening in her stomach, she answered, "Dr. Mallone here."

"Madison, it's urgent," the voice from the board crackled through the line. "There are increasing concerns over the stability of the ground around the park and immediate vicinity. We need to mobilize the evacuation now; the risk of eruption is imminent. You need to relay this strongly to everyone you speak to in the region."

"Understood," Madison replied, swallowing hard. "I'll ensure the message gets out. I'm on it, thank you."

She hung up, adrenaline coursing through her. "I just got more information from the geological board. They're escalating the threat level, and they believe an eruption could happen within hours. Everyone needs to know this is urgent. No one can afford to wait!"

The surrounding group tensed, absorbing the weight of her words. Noah stepped forward, his brow furrowing with concern. "We need to get the news out now. If the risk is that high, it's vital that every single person understands there's no time left. People should be able to figure out this mountain will not be quiet. Whoever is ready will get picked up. We have to get going!"

Madison nodded; her voice was steady yet urgent. "Let's have the schools send out alerts, and let's have the emergency services fully prepared for the growing evacuation." We need loudspeakers across the area; this news has to travel fast."

As they brainstormed, the townsfolk began gathering again, now looking to Madison and Noah for guidance. The sense of community solidarity only grew stronger in the face of adversity.

"Listen up! Everyone!" Madison called, her voice carrying over the growing crowd. "I've received word that the Yellowstone instability presents imminent danger, requiring immediate evacuation of our community." Continual seismic activity shows that we could see significant eruption events in a matter of hours."

A hush fell over the crowd as the magnitude of her words sank in. Then came the questions—anxious, frantic voices spilling out, seeking reassurance and clarity.

"What about our homes?" a worried mother asked, clutching her child tightly.

"We leave them for now," Madison replied, her gaze softening as she locked eyes with the woman. "The most important thing is that we all stay safe. After the situation stabilizes, if you have insurance, reach out—you can replace material possessions, but not lives.

"What about our pets?" another person shouted.

"Bring them!" A rush of urgency infused Madison's tone. "Get them into your vehicles if you can. Take what you need to keep them safe. We're prioritizing all living beings."

"Are there designated shelter areas?" a teenage boy called out.

"There were, but we can't use them. We are looking at the eruption of a super volcano and no human could withstand surviving in 15 feet or more of ash. Everyone needs to get off this mountain and get as far away as possible." Madison's heart was racing.

Realizing she had held the attention of the crowd; Madison took a deep breath. "We are a community, and together we will get through this. We can get to safety and regroup. Check on your family, your friends, and your neighbors. Make sure everyone is attending to the evacuation protocol."

The atmosphere shifted from despair to determination. People who had been in shock moved with newfound resolve, rallying together to aid those who needed additional support. Madison watched as families clustered together, and neighbors began checking on each other, ready to lend a hand wherever needed.

"Keep spreading the word," Madison instructed her team. Each of them headed toward different areas to ensure everyone was aware. She turned to Noah, catching his eye. "Let's assist where we can. We can't leave people in the dark."

"Absolutely," he replied, a fire igniting in his expression. "We'll make sure everyone knows the importance of leaving immediately."

They moved through the crowd, Madison taking time to reassured individuals and families as they hustled to make their preparations.

At the school, the atmosphere was frantic as volunteers organized supplies and shelter logistics. Madison felt her heart swell with pride at the kindness radiating from her community. Kids helped adults load vehicles, while others spread out to help direct traffic towards evacuation points.

"Madison!" a voice snapped her attention, and she turned to see the officer from earlier pushing through the throng. "Reports are rolling in that an evacuation alert is about to be issued regionally. We have emergency services heading out to assist us as well."

"That's excellent," Madison breathed, relief washing over her momentarily. "But we must stay ahead of the curve! We must evacuate everyone quickly before things escalate. We do not know how much time we have. Lava is flowing under our feet as we speak!"

The officer nodded; urgency palpable in his stance. "We'll get there, but we must coordinate the shelters and ensure everyone is aware."

As Madison and Noah continued to move through the school, communicating with volunteers and assuring people of the approaching evacuation, Madison's phone buzzed again. With urgency backing her, she answered, feeling the weight of responsibility settle stoutly on her shoulders.

"Dr. Mallone," the voice on the other end said hurriedly, "we're seeing continuous pressure building beneath Yellowstone. Your region needs our focus. We need a clear reevaluation of the evacuation zones based on current readings."

Madison's heart raced. "We were just briefing the local community, and everything is in motion. The focus is on immediate evacuation for everyone."

"Be sure to communicate that time is an enemy. Every moment counts!"

"Thanks," she said, her resolve hardening. As she hung up, she turned to Noah, "We need to reiterate to everyone just how crucial it is to leave right now. No more delaying, no more second-guessing. Everyone needs to get off this mountain now! We are out of time!"

"On it!" he replied, scanning the area for a place to rally the crowd again. "Let's get everyone's attention."

Noah climbed onto a low wall, raising his arms to draw the crowd together. "Everyone! Can I have your attention, please?"

Gradually, the conversations died down, and people turned to look at him. Madison joined him on the wall, her heart pounding as she surveyed the faces reflecting both fear and determination.

"Thank you all for your quick action so far," Noah began, his voice ringing with urgency. "As you've heard from Dr. Mallone and the local officials, the situation is escalating at Yellowstone. This is not just a precaution; it is essential to evacuate immediately."

Madison stepped forward; her voice was firm yet compassionate. "We are urging everyone to proceed to the nearest evacuation site—the high school or the community center—quickly and safely. Time is of the essence, and each minute spent here could put you in danger. Please leave your homes behind; our priority is your safety."

A murmur stirred through the crowd; a wave of anxiety mixed with resolve. "Do we have enough resources?" someone called from the back.

"We're coordinating with emergency services to ensure we have shelter, food, and medical help ready for everyone. Grab essential items, but leave anything replaceable behind. We need your focus on getting to safety."

"Check on your neighbors!" another person shouted, reinforcing the sentiment of community solidarity.

Madison felt the energy shift as people rallied behind the message, gathering their belongings and gathering hugs and goodbyes from family and friends.

"Let's move, people!" Noah encouraged, descending from the wall. "We can do this together!"

They broke down into teams, each focusing on specific areas to ensure everyone knew how critical the evacuation was. Madison teamed up with the same volunteers who had helped her earlier, their spirits encouraged by the camaraderie.

As they moved from house to house, Madison remembered the elderly couple from before. With a knot of anxiety forming in her stomach, she led her team toward the local market. "You think they're still here?" someone asked hesitantly.

"I hope so. They have to be somewhere nearby," she replied, her gaze scanning the lot filled with vehicles.

Inside the market, the shuffling of carts and the low hum of conversation underscored the growing sense of urgency. People lined up, grabbing essentials, oblivious to the potential danger unfolding.

"Excuse me! Does anyone here know where Mr. and Mrs. Hargrove are?" Madison called out to the shoppers. Some turned to her, confusion on their faces.

A familiar voice piped from the checkout line. "They're right over there!" A friendly face waved, pointing to the back of the store.

Relief surged through Madison as she spotted the couple near the cereal aisle. She hurried over, her heart racing with emotion. "Mr. and Mrs. Hargrove, thank goodness I found you!"

Mrs. Hargrove looked up; surprise clear in her expression. "Madison, dear! What are you doing here?"

"I came to warn you! You need to leave right now. There's a serious situation unfolding at Yellowstone, and you need to evacuate!" Madison said, urgency threading through every word.

"Evacuate? Wait a moment; we heard nothing about that!" Mr. Hargrove interjected, concern knitting his brow.

"It's true, and time is critical. You can pack essential items, but you have to rush back to the high school or community center," Madison reiterated, fear worming its way into her tone. "Please trust me; every moment is vital."

"Oh, dear!" Mrs. Hargrove exclaimed, flustered. "We did not know! We thought we'd just get a few things for the road."

Madison took their hands gently in hers. "I promise you I will replace all the food and items." Your safety can't. You must come with me right now."

The couple exchanged glances filled with concern, but nodded resolutely. "Alright, let's do it," Mr. Hargrove said, determination setting his jaw.

"Thank you!" Madison said, relief washing over her. "We'll help you get what you need."

Together, they moved through the store, Mr. and Mrs. Hargrove gathering necessities while Madison and her group supported them, moving with purpose. The urgency hung in the air like a thick fog, but there was also a growing sense of empowerment within them all. They were part of something larger than themselves.

Once everyone had what they needed, they hurried out to the parking lot, where the town continued its bustling exodus. Madison led the Hargroves toward her truck, spotting Noah in the distance as he helped load people into the bus designated for evacuation.

"Thank you for assisting us, dear," Mrs. Hargrove said as they climbed into the truck. "You've been a godsend."

"Honestly, I'm just glad I could get to you in time. The last thing I want is anyone being left behind," Madison replied, trying to keep her tone upbeat while the urgency of the situation weighed heavily on her mind.

As Madison started the engine and pulled out of the parking lot, she glanced in the rearview mirror at the chaos unfolding. Family after family poured into their cars, and the buses filled up with those needing a ride. There was an underlying sense of determination in the air, people banding together to ensure their safety.

"Which way to the school?" Mr. Hargrove asked, his voice steady but layered with concern.

"Just keep going straight and take a left at the next intersection," she instructed, her heart racing as her thoughts raced alongside the vehicle. Just then, her phone buzzed again, and she reluctantly glanced down, knowing she had to keep her focus on the road.

"Is it the board again?" Noah's voice suddenly filtered in from the backseat. He must have moved closer after helping the other passengers.

"Yes, they're checking in constantly," she said, trying to keep her cool as her thumb hovered over the screen. "They're monitoring the seismic readings live, and if anything changes, we need to be ready to react."

"We'll stay ready," Noah affirmed, scanning for further evacuation needs. "Have they updated you on the projected timeline yet?"

"Not yet. But if they think an eruption could happen imminently, we can't afford to take any chances." Madison glanced at Mr. Hargrove's worried expression in the rearview, and her heart sank for a moment. "We're doing everything we can. Just keep going."

As they pulled into the intersection, the sight of people filling the high school parking lot greeted her like a scene from a dystopian novel—a mix of fear and determination painted across weary faces. Madison parked the truck and quickly turned to the Hargroves.

"Stay close to me, okay? We'll get you settled inside, and then I need to check on what's happening in the school."

"Thank you, dear," Mrs. Hargrove replied as they climbed out of the vehicle. Volunteers filled the bustling schoolyard, directing traffic, setting up supply tents, and ensuring everyone's safety.

Madison felt a mix of frenetic energy and steadfastness as they joined the throng of people pouring into the gymnasium. Emotions charged the atmosphere inside; some people quietly conversed, and others settled in, searching for safety in the chaos.

"Let's find a place for your things," she said, looking for an appropriate corner to help the couple get organized.

"Oh, it's alright," Mr. Hargrove insisted. "We need little. Just a place to sit, and we'll manage."

Madison nodded, appreciating their resilience, and guided them closer to the centrally located supplies. "Please, make yourselves comfortable. I'll check in with the emergency coordinators, and I'll be right back."

As she maneuvered through the crowd, she spotted Noah talking to a group of volunteers, coordinating their ongoing efforts. She approached him, her heart swelling with relief to see him managing so efficiently in the chaos.

"How are things on your end?" she asked, trying to catch her breath.

"Pretty good, actually," Noah replied, excitement lacing his voice as he glanced around. "We've gotten most of the vulnerable populations in the shelter. The buses are continuing to rotate, and everyone is finally grasping the urgency. I think the coordination is holding up."

Madison felt a sense of hope rising within her, even despite the overwhelming circumstances. "That's great, but the board is saying the seismic activity is escalating rapidly. We really need to keep pushing the message out there."

"Absolutely. We should make another announcement soon. Everyone needs to stay aware," he said, surveying the crowd.

Before they could strategize further, another tremor shook the ground beneath them, causing Madison to lose her balance for a moment. Gasps erupted through the gymnasium as people instinctively clung to nearby chairs or one another.

"We can't stay here if this keeps up!" a voice called out, fear threading through the crowd once more.

Madison and Noah exchanged concerned glances, urgency coursing through them as the tremors subsided, but the tension remained potent.

"Let's take this outside—people need to be informed of what's happening," Noah urged. While outside, Noah noticed a fault near where a few people were standing. Noah ran over to them to help them move. Rocked by tremors, one man started falling into it. The next thing Noah heard was the man screaming. Noah reached the fault just in time to see the man fall into a river of lava. The man literally melted in front of Noah's eyes. "Everyone run to the buses right now! Get on the buses! Don't stop or you will die!"

As Noah led the group away from the fault, he spotted Madison. "Maddie! Get to the buses! Get everyone on the buses!"

Another tremor pulsed through the ground, more pronounced than the last, and battered walls rattled in response. Madison instinctively reached out for Noah, who quickly found her hand and squeezed it, grounding her amid the shaking chaos.

"It's happening," a voice murmured in the crowd, panic rising. "We know what to do! Everyone, follow the protocols we've established. The time to act is now!"

They moved through the throng, working as a team to direct families and individuals toward the evacuation points. Madison felt the adrenaline coursing through her veins, inspiring her resolve even more.

As everyone was loading on the buses, a loud rumble echoed from somewhere deep beneath the earth, punctuated by a sharp explosion that convulsed the ground.

"There's no time!" Madison shouted, her heart racing as she grabbed Noah's hand tightly. "Everyone, out! Move now!"

With urgency, they guided the frantic crowd toward the exit, but they could see that shock froze some people, leaving them unable to react to the surrounding chaos.

"Go! Get moving!" Noah shouted, his voice a lifeline, pulling them out of their stupor.

Madison pulled together her reserves of strength. "Stay close! We're getting you out of here! Just follow us!"

Amidst the chaos, they would need to make critical decisions—there wasn't time for everyone to gather their belongings. Some families clutched what they could, looking for direction, while others were still hesitant to leave without their things.

The tremors continued to intensify, echoing a feeling of urgency that was palpable in the air. Outside, they could hear sirens blaring as emergency vehicles raced toward them. The smell of sulfur was becoming overwhelming.

"Madison!" a voice cried, and she turned to see Eli Pearson running toward her, eyes wide. "What's happening? Is it really that bad?"

"Yes, we have a river of lava running under our feet. If we aren't out of here in seconds, we will have a big problem!" Madison yelled.

The tremors rolled through the ground again, but now they felt like distant thunder, harsh reminders of the chaos beneath their feet. With one last thrust, they rushed into the aftermath of the schoolyard, where the urgency of the evacuation was palpable. Buses were now lining up, headlights cutting through the dust and early morning light, while volunteers directed traffic, ensuring everyone could board safely. The air crackled with a palpable tension, a silent scream preceding the earth's roar. Madison, her face streaked with grime and sweat, barked orders into her headset, her voice tight with urgency. The seismic readings were off the charts, climbing exponentially; the eruption wasn't a matter of hours anymore, but minutes. Every second counted. The thermal maps pulsed, a vibrant, terrifying heartbeat on the screen, revealing the magma's relentless ascent.

"Noah, status report!" she yelled over the din of the emergency response team, her voice barely audible above the rising cacophony of sirens and panicked shouts.

Noah, his ranger uniform caked in mud and ash, fought his way through the throngs of fleeing tourists and panicked residents. The

A sea of terrified faces mirroring the surrounding chaos choked the usually tranquil pathways. The smell of sulfur was overpowering, a suffocating blanket clinging to the air, thick and acrid. The ground continued to tremble violently, each tremor a brutal reminder of the impending doom.

"Buses are ready at the designated assembly points, Madison, he yelled back, his voice strained. "But we're severely short of drivers. Many are stranded or refusing to enter the danger zone."

"We'll use whoever we can get. We need to move people out now. Every second lost means lives lost. Focus on getting the elderly and children out first. Prioritize the vulnerable," Madison responded, her eyes darting between the frantic scenes undoing around her and the ominous readings on her monitors.

Madison glanced to her left and saw an elderly couple struggling to move their belongings. Without hesitation, she sprinted toward them. "Here, let me help you!" she said, grabbing a heavy bag and hoisting it onto the bus.

"Oh, thank you, dear," Mrs. Hargrove gasped, her face flushed with anxiety. "We were worried we wouldn't make it in time."

"Just stick with us!" Madison replied cheerily, urged them onto the bus. They climbed aboard, finding a seat near the front, and she felt a rush of success.

The ground shook once more, more violently than ever before. It felt as if the earth itself was warning them, pushing them along urgently. Madison stumbled briefly but quickly regained her footing, her heart racing at the growing threat. She could notice the rising and falling of the ground. "The land is buckling; we got to move!" Just then, everyone saw the bubbling of lava where the fault was earlier.

"Load everyone, so that no one gets left behind!" Noah shouted over the rising tension.

With each passing minute, the urgency heightened. Buses filled rapidly, and Madison counted heads to ensure a complete headcount. The chaos settled slightly, but each tremor brought another wave of fear that swept through the crowd.

"Get on the buses! Leave the bags behind!" she called out again, her voice reverberating against the school walls.

Suddenly, she noticed a small group of children standing together, fear etched on their faces. Their parents were nowhere in sight.

"Hey, over here!" she said, beckoning them to her. "Where are your parents?"

"They said to wait for them, but they didn't come back!" one little girl replied, tears glistening in her eyes.

"Alright, come with me!" Madison said quickly, kneeling before them to make eye contact. "We'll get you to safety, I promise. We'll find them soon. Everyone is evacuating."

Quickly, she led the children toward the nearest bus, hurrying them inside and making sure they found places to sit. She watched as the bus driver turned to her, nodding in acknowledgment that he would monitor the children.

"Go! Get them out of here!" Madison urged, her breath catching. "We can't afford to lose anyone else. Everyone needs to move now!"

She spun back to the group of children, ensuring they felt safe. "Alright, all of you, stay close together! We've got to make sure everyone gets on."

With a last nod, she dashed back toward Noah, helping usher the last few remaining people toward safety. One by one, they clambered aboard, fear and determination clear in their quick motions.

It was a scene of unprecedented chaos. The chaos separated families. As: Occupants fled, abandoning their cars and adding to the human tide surging toward the designated assembly points. Usually pristine, the landscape was now a terrifying tableau of nature's raw power, utter pandemonium. The unrelenting forces of nature transformed the once-peaceful meadows into chaotic battlefields where humanity fought, not an enemy, but nature itself. The orderly beauty of Yellowstone National Park had vanished, replaced by an overwhelming sense of terror and chaos.

Finally, as the last bus rolled away, Madison turned to Noah, urgency clear in her gaze. "We need to ensure everyone has made it! Is there anyone left?"

"I'm sorry Maddie, these buses are not stopping. If we stop these buses to look around, we are risking the lives of everyone here we are trying to protect. We did our best." Noah gave Madison a hug, setting his chin on the top of her head, holding her tightly.

The entire mood on all the buses were silence. A few children were whimpering. The adults were stoic. Everyone knew there were people left behind. Since there were several buses, no one knew the whereabouts of family members. The first and only priority was to get everyone off of this mountain and to put as much distance from Yellowstone as possible.

Chapter 5

Hot Springs

Suddenly, an emergency alert blared from the bus's radio, cutting through the anxious murmurs among the passengers.

"Attention, all residents," the voice declared, clear yet filled with urgency. "Immediate evacuation in effect. The school has spotted lava flow. Do not approach the school. If you are receiving this message, get off the mountain. Head south. Repeat: immediate evacuation in effect. Head south."

The buses, a motley collection of yellow behemoths, were quickly filling up. They requested teachers, park staff, and even tourists with a driver's license to help. The scene was inspiring, yet also heart-wrenching; The heroic efforts to save others amid the chaos and desperation was a testament to the strength and compassion of the human spirit.

Noah, along with a small group of rangers, navigated the throngs of people, guiding them toward the buses. His voice, though hoarse, remained steady, offering reassurance and directing the flow of terrified people. He saw acts of selfless bravery:

strangers helping strangers, elderly people being carried to safety, and children comforted by volunteers. He witnessed panic, fear, and despair, but also unwavering courage, selfless acts of kindness and compassion, and an indomitable human spirit refusing to surrender in the face of imminent death.

The task was monumental. Thousands needed to be evacuated, and the window of opportunity was shrinking with every passing minute. The ground was shaking with increasing intensity, cracks appearing in the earth, swallowing everything in their path. Hot springs were erupting sporadically, spewing scalding water and steam into the already chaotic landscape. The air was thick with volcanic ash, a cloud of gritty, suffocating dust that coated everything in a layer of gray.

As the first buses pulled away, a deep rumble shook the ground, more violent than any tremor before. The sky, once a clear blue, was now darkening, a menacing shadow spreading across the landscape. The eruption was imminent. Noah, watching the first vehicles depart, felt a mixture of relief and dread. Relief that they had evacuated some dread at the sheer scale of the impending disaster and the countless lives still in danger.

The evacuation continued a frantic race against time, a struggle against the unrelenting forces of nature. The logistical challenges were immense; fuel was running low, communication lines were failing, and the roads were becoming impassable. Yet, against all odds, humanity pressed on, united by a shared fear and a desperate hope for survival.

Amidst the chaos, acts of incredible courage and selflessness emerged. Instead of fleeing for their own safety, a group of teenagers helped direct traffic, guiding stranded drivers to safe routes. A retired park ranger, despite his age, worked tirelessly to help evacuate elderly people and children. A family of tourists, realizing the gravity of the situation, shared their food and water with others. These acts of bravery and kindness, small sparks of humanity amid the overwhelming chaos, brought a glimmer of hope in this dark hour.

The sky darkened further, and the air grew heavy with the smell of sulfur and ash. A faint red glow appeared on the horizon, a terrifying precursor to the eruption. Panicked cries mingled with the roar of escaping steam and the cracking earth as the ground trembled more violently. The last buses were struggling to navigate the increasingly treacherous landscape as the first signs of the eruption became visually apparent. The race against time was far from over, but the clock was ticking down. Noah and Madison knew that whatever happened, they had done all they could. Now, they faced the consequences, the raw and unconquerable might of nature.

As the bus meandered forward, the landscape transformed. What had once been lush greenery was now marred by smoke and dust, signaling the encroaching disaster. Even in the dark, they saw heated vapors rising from the ground in the distance.

Madison and Noah took turns checking on the passengers, ensuring that everyone was secure and accounted for. They walked through the aisles, speaking with families, offering reassurances they would be safe. The fear in the eyes of the children was palpable, and Madison kneeled beside each one, delivering gentle words of comfort.

"Hey there," she said to a little girl clutching a stuffed animal tightly. "What's your name?"

"Emily," the girl whispered, glancing up at her through tears. "I'm scared."

"I understand, Emily. It's okay to feel scared. But look around! You're not alone; we're all here together, and we're going to get you to safety," Madison reassured her, giving her a warm smile.

Emily managed a small smile back, gripping her stuffed animal a little tighter but looking slightly less fearful.

"That's it! Just hold on to that teddy bear," Madison continued, glancing around at other parents doing the same with their children. "We are strong together, and soon we'll be safe in a shelter."

Noah was nearby, helping an elderly couple. He was speaking to them in calm tones as they settled into their seats, and Madison felt a rush of gratitude for his presence. They were a team, and together they could make a difference.

After Madison confirmed every passenger was on the bus, she returned to her seat beside Noah. "So, what's next?" she asked, looking through the window at the smoke on the horizon.

"We'll stay in contact with emergency services and any updates from the geological board. Get off this God forsaken mountain." Noah was at a loss for words.

"Absolutely," Madison replied, her mind racing with the many tasks awaiting them. "We also need to establish a way to account for all evacuees, ensuring no one gets separated from their family or caregivers. I want everyone to sign a sign-in sheet."

As they continued down the road, the surroundings shifted again; the terrain becoming more rugged and the distant mountains looming large. From the bus's window, the thick gray clouds above the park pressed against the sky as if calling attention to the impending disaster.

"We're entering the outskirts of Cody now," Noah said, peering out the front windshield.

But as they approached town, a chill crept into Madison's belly. Emergency vehicles raced past, their sirens blaring, adding urgency to their mission. Large plumes of smoke rose in the distance, blackening the sky—an ominous foreshadowing of the chaos yet to come.

"Look at that!" someone cried out from the back of the bus, pointing out the window.

Madison turned to see what they were all pointing at—distant flames licking the sky, a surreal sight against the darkening horizon. The situation was deteriorating faster than anyone had expected.

Tremors continued as the buses were driving as fast as they could safely. The noise of the wailing children quieted as her voice engaged them, and adults focused on the message instead of the chaos. The fear was still palpable but was slowly being replaced by a sense of determination.

"Stay with me, Emily!" Madison said firmly. "We'll be alright. Just breathe deeply, okay?"

Emily nodded; her wide eyes filled with tears as she looked to Madison for reassurance.

"Remember, we're in this together," Madison continued, reminded herself as much as Emily. "We'll stay calm, and we'll find our way through this."

The tremors gradually subsided, the buses continued their southward journey.

Madison was sitting next to Noah, trying to figure out their next move. We need to leave before she blows. I don't know where we'll end up. I'm thinking we can find an enormous cave. We'll be safe in that as long as we are away from the park. This eruption will keep chasing us further and further away. I wish we could get out of this area, but the ash will clog the vehicles before we could get away." Madison needed to come up with a plan.

Madison shook her head. "Noah, where are we going to find a cave system? If we had one without lava tubes, that might just work. It would protect us from the ash until we can make it to the east coast. It's going to get very ugly."

Noah gave Madison a soft kiss on the top of her head. "Let me talk to the driver. I know such a place." With a big smile on his face, Noah went to speak to the bus driver.

The bus continued to lurch forward, and Madison looked back at the scene behind them. The ash cloud bobbed ominously above, and within seconds, they could see flames bursting forth from the ground, licking angrily at the sky. Panic surged through her, filling her veins with dread. "This is really happening," she whispered.

"Keep your heads down and stay calm!" the driver shouted, navigating the rocky terrain as they raced out of the chaos. Gripping the seat, Madison's heart pounded as her mind raced through every scenario they had trained for.

"We'll make it," Noah insisted. "We have to. Those caves are the only hope we have of surviving the fallout from the eruption."

Just then, the bus jolted violently as it hit a bump, and the driver veered, narrowly avoiding a fissure opening in the road. The chaos of the seismic activity transformed the surrounding landscape into a scene from a nightmare—trees cracked and fell, deep cracks snaked through the ground, and the distant roar of Yellowstone echoed like a monster awakening.

"Stay alert!" the driver shouted, glancing in the rearview mirror, the tension evident in his voice. "They're saying the ash will be hot, and the roads may not hold up for long!"

Madison glanced out the window, her heart racing at the devastation unfolding. The landscape that had once been green and vibrant was now dark and foreboding. Signs warned of unstable ground, and the sky filled with swirling ash blocked out the moonlight, casting the world into shadows.

They needed to find safety quickly. As the bus careened down the road, Madison's mind raced with the enormity of the task ahead. The air thick with swirling ash was suffocating, growing hotter with each passing moment. She turned to Noah, his expression focused, but concern creased his brow.

"Do you think we'll make it to the caves in time?" Madison asked, her voice barely above a whisper, overwhelmed by the urgency of their situation.

"We have to," Noah replied, determination fueling his response. "It's the only chance we have. If we can reach the caves, we'll survive the ash fallout and any potential lava flow." Noah reached out and grabbed Madison into his arms, kissing her gently.

"I've wanted to do this for such a long time. I will protect you Madison, I swear it."

"I believe you Noah." She felt so safe in his arms. Never had Madison felt so safe. Standing there, she just wanted to melt into his arms.

The bus swerved to avoid yet another large crack forming in the road. Fragments of debris pelted against the sides of the vehicle, and the driver cursed under his breath, gripping the wheel. "Hang on back there!" he shouted, focusing intently on the road ahead.

The other buses following them were zig-zagging too, following their tracks successfully.

Madison turned back toward the passengers, a mix of fear and resolve filling her. "Everyone, stay calm! We're doing everything we can to get you safe! Let's keep each other together!"

The sound of the engine roared, drowning out the tremors beneath them, but the vibrations made it clear they were still in danger. She looked out the window, seeing the fiery glow illuminating the skyline in the far distance, a reminder of the immense power that lay beneath the earth.

Behind them, the chaos of the park grew louder, shouts mingling with the wailing of sirens. As the bus approached a fork in the road, the driver made a quick decision. "I can take you to the caves, but we must go a rough route to avoid the flooding! Hold on tight!"

"No!" she gasped. "What if it leads to more instability?"

"Trust me; it's our best shot," he replied firmly, and with that, the driver took the left path, veering away from the main roads.

The bus jolted violently over the bumpy terrain, and Madison held her breath, feeling the tension rise in her chest. She glanced back at Danny and his mother, who were clinging to one another. "We're almost there!" she reassured them, though she wasn't sure how to gauge that statement.

They bounced along the rough road, the sound of rocks and mud hitting the underside echoing ominously. The bus slowed momentarily as the driver maneuvered around a deep gully. Madison felt a wave of relief as they passed through relative safety.

"That was a close one!" one passenger exclaimed, laughter mingling with disbelief.

"Just keep your eyes on the road!" Noah urged from the front, trying to lighten the mood.

As they continued, the ground shook more violently, signaling the impending danger. "Let's hold on!" the driver yelled, gripping the wheel tightly as he pushed the bus forward.

Madison's heart pounded in her chest. The surrounding ground lit up with a fiery glow as they neared the shadows of the mountain caves that promised refuge. The air grew hotter, thick with dust and ash, as they rounded a bend and saw the mouth of a cave up ahead—a dark entrance beckoning them forward. Madison ended up falling asleep with her head resting on Noah's chest. It was the best sleep she had in a very long time.

Chapter 6

Entrance

Another hour of careful driving finally reaching Jewel Cave. It so happened that this cave was the third largest cave system in the country. Scientists believe it could actually be the largest, because the system's vastness prevents full exploration. The wind gusts inside the cave evidenced further chambers beyond those explored.

"There!" Madison pointed excitedly. "That's the cave entrance! We need to make it!"

"Everyone, brace yourselves!" the driver yelled as he revved the engine one last time, propelling them toward the entrance with a surge of speed.

They barreled through the mouth of the cave just as a powerful tremor shook the ground. The bus jolted, bouncing as they entered the darkened space. Dust and small rocks fell from the ceiling as the driver wrestled to maintain control, pulling the bus to a halt as they landed inside the cave.

As the dust settled, a collective sigh of relief echoed from the passengers. The cave formed a deep pocket, offering dark, open ground that seemed to provide a temporary safety shield from the chaos outside.

"Everyone out! Move quickly!" the driver instructed as the passengers scrambled to gather their belongings and disembark from the bus.

Madison took a deep breath, realizing they had made it. "Get down the stairs and head deep into the cave! We need to stay away from the entrance in case of more slides!" she called, guiding families back as they came through the cave's entrance.

"Danny! Stay close to me!" she yelled, spotting the young boy rounding the corner with his mother.

Once they were all safely inside, the group quickly settled in, gathering to assess their situation. The cave felt damp and echoed, but there was a sense of security in being out of direct danger for the moment.

"Is everyone alright?" Madison asked, scanning the group for any signs of distress. The nervous energy still tinged the air, but a few families started chatting amongst themselves, drawing comfort from the presence of others.

"We have to regroup and figure out what comes next," Noah said, stepping close to her.

Madison nodded, her heart still racing from the recent chaos, but a flicker of determination ignited within her. "Right. We need to assess resources and make sure everyone checks in."

The flickering lights from their flashlights illuminated the cave's rocky surfaces, casting elongated shadows that danced ominously on the walls. Families huddled together, whispering to each other, but there was also a palpable sense of camaraderie as they realized they were in this together. There were staircases that went in every direction. The main hall of the cave entrance was very tall, with a chilly breeze, and felt so welcoming to this group of nomads.

"Let's create a medical area," Madison suggested, holding up her flashlight to attract attention. "If everyone can gather here, we can take a headcount, distribute supplies, and help anyone who needs it. I would suggest keeping the seniors near here."

A few volunteers quickly nodded and gathered the families toward a relatively flat area in the back of the cave where the light was brighter. Madison clapped her hands to encourage cooperation. "Alright, everyone! Please remain calm, and we'll get through this together. Let's do a quick headcount and make sure no one is missing."

As groups coalesced, Danny's mother approached, her face still pale but tinged with relief. "Thank you for looking out for him. "I became scared when he wandered off," she said, her voice quivering.

Madison offered her a warm smile. "I'm just glad we found him in time. He's a brave little superhero."

"Thank you," she replied, her tension easing as she hugged Danny tighter. He grinned up at Madison, the worry momentarily forgotten.

Once everyone had gathered, Noah stepped up to aid Madison in organizing the headcount. "Alright, let's do this quickly. Raise your hand when your name is called and let's keep the lines clear!"

One by one, they called out names, confirming who was present, and a sense of relief washed over Madison as she marked off each family. The atmosphere felt less frantic, tempered by the shared experience and the knowledge that they were no longer on shaky ground—at least for now.

However, the growing sound of distant eruptions that echoed inside the cave reminded them that the danger was far from over. The tremors continued intermittently, and the ground was still shifting, leaving everyone hyper-aware of their surroundings.

"We need to be ready for additional tremors," Madison warned, once the headcount was complete. "Keep your belongings close, and if you feel the ground shake, don't panic—just find a solid structure to hold on to. Someone bolted these ramp walkways into the rock, so I'm sure they are safe. This is great shelter for us."

One volunteer raised their hand and spoke up. "What about the air quality? It's filling with ash—I worry about respiratory issues!"

Madison nodded, heart racing again at the mention of the ash. "We need to carve out a small section for those who might have trouble breathing. If you have masks, please make them available. We also need to ensure everyone has enough water and any medical supplies. Jewel Cave is a very, very big cave system. I just have us here to rest a bit. We are going to have to go much deeper for total protection."

As they worked to divvy up resources, increasing apprehension filled the cave. The echoes of distant eruptions continued to rumble ominously, and wisps of dust floated into the air through the cave entrance.

"Noah, I think we should send out a small team to scout for more supplies and connections to nearby shelters," Madison suggested, glancing over at him. "We may need to prepare for a longer stay, depending on what happens."

"Absolutely," Noah replied decisively. "We'll need an experienced team familiar with the area and a plan for potential routes back down to safety. There are rivers in this cave system, so we will have a fresh water supply and probably fish, too."

Madison turned to the group, raising her voice above the chatter. "I need volunteers who know the area well and can help with scouting for any additional resources or routes. We want to ensure we're prepared for whatever comes next!"

A few hands shot up, and within moments, a small group of volunteers was ready to support the effort. Noah led them outside the cave entrance cautiously while Madison remained behind to manage those settling in.

While monitoring the children, she encouraged them to share games and activities peacefully. "Let's play a game of imagination! Everyone pick a hero you want to be. What hero powers do you want to have?" she prompted, encouraged them to weave stories together.

As their imaginations blossomed amidst the heaviness of survival, a wave of quiet optimism washed over Madison. Just then, she saw Noah return, his expression serious as he stepped into the cave.

"Madison," he said, his voice low but urgent. "The explosions are getting closer. We need to prepare everyone for the possibility of moving again shortly. I don't think we can stay at the cave entrance for long."

Fear prickled along Madison's spine at his words. "How much time do we have?"

"Not long," Noah replied, tension tightening his features. "We need to relay the risks clearly and ensure everyone is ready to go at a moment's notice. We can't let anyone linger if the ash comes in here."

"Okay, let's gather everyone's attention!" Madison called out to the group, her heart pounding as she felt the gravity of the situation once more.

"Everyone, please, I need your attention!" Madison shouted, her voice cutting through the chatter as the families turned to look at her, expressions ranging from curiosity to anxiety.

"We need to go deeper into the cave. The seismic activity is increasing, and we want to ensure everyone is prepared to hurry," she said, making sure her tone conveyed urgency without inciting panic.

"Gather your essential belongings now! Ensure everyone is with their families—we cannot afford to leave anyone behind," Noah added, stepping closer to her to lend support.

Whispers of concern spread through the tent, and families began hurriedly collecting their things. Madison could see mothers whispering to their children, ensuring they stayed close. She felt

Danny tugging on her hand and turned to him with a reassuring smile.

"Are we going to be, okay?" he asked softly, his innocent worry piercing her heart.

"Absolutely, we are going to be okay," she replied confidently, squeezing his hand. "Just stay with me, and we'll find a way through this together."

As families gathered their essentials, Madison circulated through the tent, assisting anyone who looked uncertain. She offered encouraging words and reassurances, knowing that their emotional state was just as important as their physical safety right now.

The volunteers worked with renewed urgency, checking supplies and coordinating efforts as they prepared for the worst. Madison glanced at the cave entrance, noting the growing shadows outside as night fell deeper, thick ash clouds reminiscent of stormy weather rolled ominously overhead.

"Let's make sure the younger kids understand what's happening," she said to Noah, who had been helping with the supplies. "If they're involved in our planning, they might feel a little less anxious."

"Noah!" Lucas called from across the tent, his voice wavering.

"I'm right here, Lucas!" Noah replied, moving towards the small boy. "What do you need?"

"I want to help! Let me help!" Lucas insisted, bouncing on his feet.

"Of course, buddy," Madison said, her heartwarming at his eagerness. "You can help by making sure everyone knows to check in with the volunteers. Every bit counts."

With the evacuation preparations underway, the atmosphere felt increasingly tense. The sound of distant explosions rattled the ground again, and the cave walls trembled ominously. Madison could feel the unease rising, but she held onto the belief that their community spirit would pull them through.

"Alright, everyone!" she called out again, her voice firm. "If we need to move, please stay together! Look for the nearest volunteer or family member to guide you. We will stick together every step of the way."

Just then, the emergency coordinator stepped back into the tent, another urgent expression on her face. "We've just received further updates. The geological board believes imminent eruptions are likely."

"Fifteen minutes?!" a woman cried out, fear breaking through the calm they had worked so hard to maintained.

"Yes, but remember, we will not be alone in this. We'll act quickly," the coordinator assured. "Get your families organized and make sure you have everything you need for the next leg of our journey. We'll head through the deeper caves nearby if conditions worsen."

Madison felt time slipping away as she directed families once more, trying to maintain order amidst the rising panic. "Focus! We will account for every single person! If anyone is unsure of their belongings, just gather nearby. We'll help each other through this!"

As people moved, Madison spotted Danny again and kneeled down. "Danny, stay close to your family and make sure no one wanders off. Can you help me?"

"I will!" he declared, his youthful determination shining through. "Let's do this!"

With time running out, Noah and Madison executed their plans dynamically, ensuring the families were prepared to evacuate swiftly. They communicated the routes while distributing emergency supplies.

Madison felt a sense of purpose solidifying within her as every second ticked closer to their evacuation. "We can do this!" she encouraged everyone, her heart uplifted by the communal spirit of resolve. "Together, we'll navigate through this!"

Just then, the ground shook again, more violently than before. Dust poured down from the cave ceiling, and panic surged through the crowd once more.

"Everyone, MOVE!" Noah shouted. "Down the steps! Now!"

Family units quickly organized themselves, moving toward the main exit of the cave. Madison kept close to Danny, urging him along with his family.

"Stay close to me!" she called to him as they approached the entrance, the roiling clouds of ash growing closer and heavier in the air.

As Madison helped facilitate the needs of the families, she caught sight of a commotion among the group. A woman, looking pale and shaken, was clutching her stomach, wheezing. "I don't feel well," she murmured, dropping to her knees.

"Get the medical team!" Madison shouted, rushing to her side as panic surged within her. "What's wrong? Can you tell me?"

"I—I think I inhaled too much ash earlier," the woman gasped, her eyes widening in fear.

"Get her some water and clear air!" Noah yelled to nearby volunteers. "Someone needs to assist with a first-aid kit!"

Madison quickly kneeled next to the woman, trying to keep her calm. "Breathe slowly, all right? In and out—focus on the rhythm of your breath," she instructed, her voice steady, though her insides felt twisted with concern.

The surrounding commotion escalated as more families gathered, worried glances exchanged among the crowd. "We're going to help you, I promise," Madison said, squeezing the woman's arm gently. "Stay with us—you're going to be okay."

Moments later, the medical volunteers arrived, quickly assessing her condition. Madison remained close, providing reassurance as they worked to stabilize the woman and address her needs.

"Get some fresh air into her lungs—pack those filters on!" one medic ordered, guiding more volunteers to gather supplies.

"Are we going to make it?" Danny asked, instinctively sensing the heightened tension.

"We'll get through this," Madison reassured him, kneeling to meet his gaze. "Remember, we're superheroes—we never give up, right?"

"Right!" Danny responded, puffing out his chest, a flicker of bravery shining through his worry.

"Alright, everyone! Let's move!" Noah shouted.

Madison instructed the group to be careful about breathing in the ash. The ash is very fine particles that adhere to the alveoli in the lungs. It's turned the lungs into glass. The best way Madison found to protect the group is to wrap wet clothing around the face. The water creates a strong filter, and it is fairly easy to breathe through it. Once everyone gets deeper into the cave, the ash will become less and less, transporting them to the land of damp and darkness.

The Coasts

There was no doubt the United States had it worse. While this was a world-wide event, the United States was going to have a very difficult decade. This disaster affected every square inch and every person in the U.S. President Johnson was on point and had volumes of executive orders signed before the first ash flake hit the sky. The first executive order was executing NYSE Rule 49 suspended trading during a national emergency. This rule aimed to shut down the market for up to 10 days during the emergency; however, this has yet to be tested. If the president allowed trading to keep going on, the stock market would have fallen through the floor and there would have been a run on banks. It was bad enough the country was going to be experiencing a decade of hell. Staving off a crushing depressing was paramount.

It was a sobering newscast later that night when the news reported expecting the deaths of 100,000 deaths in the "kill zone." The newscast popularized the term "kill zone." It is the 100-mile radius around Yellowstone. In the following days, rainfall tapers off, and immediately plunged into a drought. Rivers and streams dried up. There were many public service announcements showing the public how to create a filter over the air intake of the automobile. Some were using facemasks and one creative person was using coffee filters. Unfortunately, the cars still weren't moving because a week after Yellowstone erupted, most gas station pumps were empty. The major reason for this is the truckers could not drive from the refineries to the gas stations. Electricity was also spotty, and this did not help the situation either.

President Johnson had to suspend all air and rail travel in the continental states. The ash was too dangerous and could clog the engines. On June 4, 1982, a British Airways, Flight 9 going to

Perth had an experience where all four engines on the 747 flamed out.

The pilots and the passengers noted an electric purple haze surround the plane. The plan ultimately regained three engines before landing, but the pilots and the passengers were at a loss for what caused this spectacle. It turned out to be St. Elmo's Fire. St. Elmo's Fire occurs where there are storms in the vicinity. There were no storms, and the radar was clear. After the plane landed, investigators examined the Royal Royce engines and noted there was ash and pumice inside. The eruption of Mt. Galunggung and the ash that was in the upper atmosphere caused this. We could expect these same conditions worldwide for up to a year.

The ash is going to be catastrophic in a 1,000-mile area around Yellowstone. The ash will reach and impact the East Coast. They will only get 1-3 mm of ash, but that is enough to cause damage to cars and the respiratory tracts of the masses.

The basic standards of life will be affected. Experts predict billions of people will die within several years. The infrastructure will collapse and become clogged with refugees. Widespread famine will result from the contamination of water supplies by ash, severe power outages, plummeting temperatures, and the disruption of agricultural production.

When Yellowstone finally erupted, a 10.0 quake hit Los Angeles, traveling along the faults to San Francisco. There was no way help could reach California to assist and bring supplies. Planes could not fly, driving and trains were not a source either. By the time help from the east came, hundreds of thousands of people died and most of the cities burned to the ground. There were earthquakes and eruptions all along the ring-of-fire. Japan, Turkey, Pakistan, and many other countries were badly

The only way the rescuers on the east coast could get to the west coast of the country was by boat, and even that has challenges of its own. There was no way the government could provide rescue food and supplies, as transportation was non-existent.

What the public did not know is there are 20 super-volcanos in the world. Three of them are in the continental U.S. Yellowstone comprises two magma bodies. Rhyolite, a high-silica rock measuring 5.5 miles long and 25 miles wide, composes the shallow magma body. The larger body is 4-1/2 times larger and is mostly solid basalt. While most of the damages that will occur will happen in the west. There are many people who will survive and it is the people who hid in the caves. The caves will keep the waters fresh and the cold air fresh and ash free. These people will not have a peaceful time, but they will live.

The east coast had 1-3 mm of ash. While the rest of the country had much more, the east coast couldn't deal very well with the little ash they received. Because of the ash, the temperature dropped. One thing about the east coast is they are sun lovers. Cities such as Orlando depend on the tourists and the theme parks. There was no demand for people to walk around the gray skies, getting coated and walking among ash. No one was going out to eat, couldn't afford vacations, and had no desire to visit the tourist traps. The economy on the east coast was going into the crapper. America depended on the east coast to hold the country together, but it wasn't happening. Things got so bad the NFL had to suspend football games and the Super Bowl because more than half of the teams were under ash. There was no way teams could play, and even if they could, no one wanted to sit in an ash coated stadium.

President Johnson really tried his hardest to keep the country together. Civil unrests were happening daily. The unemployment rate was 22%. The only demands the public had were the desire for food. All agricultural places were affected. There was no produce. Instead of growing outdoors, many people started growing produce indoors. People who were living hand to mouth we growing in their apartments and in basements. People with more funds were growing hydroponically. Indoor growing became the rage. Most people grew beans for the protein content. People needed protein.

The population thought the answer to the needed protein thought hunting and fishing were the answer. There was not a worse idea. People considered any place with a tree a hunting ground. If it wasn't so sad, it would have been funny. Hundreds of thousands of men walking around trees looking to bag a deer or catch a fish. There was no population of deer to keep up with this demand, even if the hunters saw them. People settled with squirrels and, soon, rats. Rats no longer were a problem as they graced many dinner tables.

The clocks on civilization went back 100 years. Cars could not drive, even if special filters that stopped the clogging of the air intake. There was no gas and no hope of gas for the next couple of years. If a vehicle needed parts, they were not available. Roads: Roads were empty; people used bicycles or walked. The lucky few had horses. The only group who did not experience a change in their lifestyle was the Amish.

Crime was up. Thieves murdered people for a loaf of bread. Banks were only open one or two days a week. The banks canceled credit cards. Cash was king. If you had no cash, there was no shopping.

The sad thing was the east coast had it all. Those trapped in the west could only dream about how nice it was in the west.

Chapter 8

Mount Pleasant

Madison felt a warmth spread through her chest, glancing around to ensure families were settling in. The group had followed their instructions, staying organized amidst the chaos. But as she moved through the tents, another loud rumble echoed outside, the ground shaking angrily beneath them.

"Everyone, stay low and remain calm!" the emergency coordinator called from the center of the tent. "We are experiencing heightened seismic activity and have monitored reports of a potential eruption!"

Families responded, moving to ensure they had their necessary items as beds and supplies unfolded in a chaotic array. Despite the hard metal of the walkways and steps, everyone made themselves comfortable.

Chaos erupted once more, and another strong tremor rattled through the ground, followed by the ominous roar of the earth. The people inside the tent panicked, some stumbling backward as the shadows darkened by the entrance flickered threateningly.

The first tremors that shook the ground outside felt like a giant's playful nudge inside the cave. But as the earth continued to convulse, the playful nudge transformed into a violent shaking that rattled the very bones of the earth. Inside Jewel Cave, the air hung heavy and still, a stark contrast to the chaos raging above. Noah, his face illuminated by the weak beam of his headlamp, led the small group of survivors deeper into the labyrinthine network of tunnels. Madison, her usually composed demeanor replaced by a grim determination, followed close behind, her geologist's mind already assessing the cave's structural integrity against the onslaught of the eruption.

Behind them, a heterogeneous group of survivors shuffled along – a young family huddled together for warmth and comfort, an elderly couple leaning heavily on each other, their faces etched with a mixture of fear and exhaustion, and a young, athletic man whose wiry frame belied a surprising strength and calmness. The air was thick with the smell of damp earth and something else, something acrid and unfamiliar, a subtle hint of the volcanic fumes making their way even into the depths of the cave.

The cave was a symphony of dripping water, a constant percussion that echoed through the vast chambers, amplifying the tension. Each drip was a tiny reminder of the relentless forces of nature above, a stark counterpoint to the relative quietude of their subterranean refuge. The uneven surface of the cave floor, a treacherous mixture of slick mud and loose rocks, demanded careful footing. One misstep could send a person tumbling into the darkness, a fall with potentially fatal consequences in the unforgiving confines of the cave.

"Everyone down! Take cover!" a voice shouted from the back, and in an instant, many people dropped to the ground, seeking the support of their loved ones.

"Stay calm!" Noah called out again. "Stay low and cover your heads! We'll get through this!"

Madison felt her stomach twist with fear, but forced herself to breathed deeply. "Just keep pressing your backs against the walls! Keep everyone together!" she instructed, hoped to instill a sense of calm in the chaos.

The sudden declaration sent a wave of panic through the crowd again, mothers clinging tightly to their children and families grasping for each other. "Keep it together, everyone!" Madison shouted, maintained her composure despite her own racing heart. "We need to hurry! Remember, everything we practiced!"

Noah sat beside her; tension was visible in the way his jaw tightened. "I can't shake the feeling that this is far from over," he muttered.

"I know," Madison replied, acknowledging the fear lurking in her own heart. "But we just need to focus on what we can control right now."

Inside the cave, a stillness enveloped them, contrasting with the chaos happening outside. The air was cool and damp, providing a momentary reprieve, but the low rumble of distant earthquakes served as an ever-present reminder of their precarious situation.

"Good idea," Madison responded, scanning the darkened space. "We should monitor the little ones, especially. They might get scared in this darkness."

As they started directing families deeper into the cavern, Madison felt a sense of urgency. Anxiety lurked just beneath the surface as she felt the earth shifting outside, and the distant sound of collapsing trees echoed through the cave's entrance.

"Everyone, please stay together and find a place to settle. The medical team will check in with you shortly," she said, maintained a calm demeanor to reassured those around her. "And if you or someone you know is feeling unwell, please let us know immediately."

Danny's small hand slipped into hers again as they began navigating further into the cave. He looked up at her, his youthful expressions shifting from fear to curiosity. "What's it like in here, Madison? Will we be safe?"

"Yes, Danny," Madison assured him, kneeling down to meet his gaze. "This cave will protect us from the ash and give us shelter until we're sure it's safe to move again. Remember, superheroes look out for each other. We'll all stay brave together."

He nodded, a glimmer of courage lighting his eyes. They moved deeper into the cave, where shadows danced against the walls, forming mysterious shapes. Madison glanced back toward Noah, who was helping guide families to set up areas for themselves.

As the minutes ticked by, the sensation of claustrophobia settled in. The cave felt both like a bunker and a prison, shutting them away from the dangers outside but also trapping them amid uncertainty.

Madison returned to check on the progresses made by the medical team, which had set up a small triage station at the far end of the cave. A few volunteers were sorting through medical supplies while nurses tended to those who had arrived with injuries or respiratory issues.

"Stay aware of the ash's impact," one nurse said, monitoring a child who was coughing during his examination. "Make sure everyone is aware; we need to protect ourselves from inhaling anything harmful."

"Absolutely," Madison replied, her mind running on all the tasks still before them. "We'll make sure that at-risk individuals receive masks by regularly checking in with their families."

They had just established a rhythm when another loud rumble resonated through the cave, shaking the very walls. Dust and small pebbles rained down from the ceiling, and fearful gasps erupted from the families huddled together.

"Stay calm!" Noah shouted again; the urgency apparent in his voice. "Take cover against the walls!"

Madison dropped to the ground, instinctively protecting Danny and looking around to make sure others were safe. She could feel her heart pounding in her chest, fear creeping back in as she clutched the boy closer.

Once the tremors subsided, Madison quickly pushed herself back up. "Everyone, stay low and check on each other! Let's check everyone for injuries! She could see that the children were frightened but remained quiet, holding onto their parents and one another.

As the coordinator relayed updates to the volunteers, Madison sensed that act of unity among families within the cave—everyone sharing resources and focusing on survival despite the uncertainty that still loomed outside.

Another tremor rumbled through the cave, causing everyone to crouch lower instinctively. The ground felt alive beneath them, and Madison could see the fear in the eyes of the children as they gripped their parents tightly.

"Stay focused, everyone! This is what we've prepared for!" Noah shouted, his voice cutting through the apprehension. "We're together, and we're going to make it through this!"

Madison took a deep breath, channeling her own fear into a resolute calm. "That's right! Let's take this one step at a time. If anyone needs anything—food, water, or medical help—please let us know!"

She moved through the crowd, checking on families and ensuring that the medical volunteers had access to those who required care. The atmosphere inside the cave felt tense but resolute, as community members clung to one another, sharing snippets of comfort to ease the strain set upon them.

"Danny," she whispered, crouching near him, "how are you feeling?"

"I'm okay," he replied, his eyes reflecting the faint light of the cave. "But I can't hear my friends, and I think they're scared."

Madison nodded, understanding his concern. "Let's find your friends and bring them here with us. They'll feel better if they're together with you."

With Danny leading the way, they navigated through the clustered groups, searching for familiar faces amid the shadows deep in the cave. As they walked, Madison glanced toward the cave entrance, watching the ash whip around in the wind outside, a constant reminder of the danger enveloping them.

Finally, they stumbled upon a small group of children huddled together, their expressions a mixture of worry and confusion. "We found you!" Danny shouted, breaking their despondency.

"Danny! We feared for Danny! One boy cried, relief flooding his face as he rushed forward to join his friend.

"Stay together," Madison encouraged, ensuring the group felt protected as they clustered around her again. "You're all superheroes; remember that!"

As they returned toward the central area, another tremor rattled through the cave, accompanied by the sound of distant explosions echoing across the horizon. Dust and small pebbles fell from above, and everyone instinctively looked upward, bracing for whatever might come next.

"Everyone, check in with your family members! We need to keep our lines of communication open!" Madison called out, keeping her tone steady.

"Look!" one volunteer pointed towards the cave entrance, their features caught in the shadows of orange light glowing from outside.

"Is that..." someone began, but gasps filled the space as they caught glimpses of massive billowing clouds of ash and smoke, transforming the landscape into a swirling maelstrom of destruction.

Madison stepped closer to Noah, fear creeping through her, but resolved not to let it take hold. "What should we do if this gets worse? We might need to find another exit."

"We'll stay alert. If we have to evacuate again, we'll ensure we're ready. But for now, we need to hold our ground," Noah reassured her, his grip firm on her shoulder.

Another tremor rocked the cave, this one more intense than before, sending waves of dust cascading from the ceiling. "Get low! Cover your heads!" Madison shouted, urged children to crouch down.

As the tremors subsided, a sense of calm emerged through the atmosphere again—albeit frail and vulnerable.

The emergency coordinator turned back to the crowd. It is necessary to assess the severity of the situation outside. We're still monitoring reports, but things could escalate in a matter of minutes. We need to plan how we will leave if we have to.

Madison had to calm the group." Guys, a super volcano is going to blow. There is going to be near constant earthquakes if you haven't noticed. We are in the safest spot possible. If we go outside, we die. The buses are useless because the ash will clog the motors and we can't go anywhere without dying. It's scary, but there is life here."

"It's vital to stay together as families and have those lines of communication firmly established," Madison stressed, looking around the cave and then at the coordinator. "Let's create designated areas for families to check in and establish procedures for evacuating if necessary."

Some volunteers eagerly stepped forward, ready to help set up areas. Madison quickly organized them into groups, ensuring they remained united while reinforcing the plan of action.

"Keep your families close, stay attentive, and we will get through this," she called out, her voice a steady beacon in the turmoil. Madison's heart surged with pride and gratitude for the community's unyielding spirit.

And then the cave itself rumbled ominously around them, the ground shifting aggressively beneath their feet. The sound of the earth screeching was deafening, followed by the loud rumble of whatever lay hidden deeper within Yellowstone.

Madison felt the fear rising again but steadied herself, reaching for Danny and another nearby child to reaffirm their safety. "We will be brave together! We've made it this far, and we will not stop now!"

More trembling echoed through the cave, making the air feel thick with tension. Families looked to one another, fear flickering in their eyes, but they appeared ready to comply with Madison's instructions. The sense of communal strength was tangible, pushing them all forward despite the uncertainty.

Madison felt a sense of fortitude rising within her as she glanced at the kids clinging to their parents and at the determined faces of those near her. Together, they represented something powerful—an unwillingness to back down when faced with overwhelming odds.

Madison took charge, moving around the tent and guiding families toward the deeper area of the cave. "Please follow the volunteers! Stay with your families!"

More tremors surged through the cave, this one fiercer than before, causing everyone to feel the urgency of their situation. Mounted panic filled the air, but Madison pushed forward, keeping her focus steady as she guided families into the depths of the cave.

Once everyone settled further in, a slight calm washed over the group, though the tension remained distinctly palpable. The rocks shielded them somewhat, only amplifying the distant sounds of the chaotic eruptions outside.

At last, there was silence in the cave. The children and the parents fell asleep with the gentle rocking of the earthquakes. Noah was certain everyone passed out from sheer exhaustion.

Chapter 9

Disoriented

The group moved slowly, their headlamps cutting narrow swaths through the oppressive darkness. The cave's ambiance was both captivating and terrifying: stalactites and stalagmites, sculpted by millennia of dripping water, reached towards each other like silent, ancient sentinels. They were beautiful, yet their imposing presence felt ominous in the face of the impending disaster. Their heavy breaths, the occasional scraping of shoes against rock, and the relentless drip, drip, drip of water punctuated the silence. The darkness pressed in on them, a tangible weight against their shoulders, amplifying the feeling of isolation and vulnerability.

Madison, ever the scientist, examined a fissure in the cave wall, her headlamp illuminating a faint shimmer of heat radiating from within. "The magma's closer than I thought," she muttered, her voice was barely a whisper. "The heat is penetrating even this far down."

Noah, ever the pragmatist, nodded grimly. "We need to find a stable, spacious chamber – somewhere safe to wait this out." He glanced back at the survivors, their faces reflecting the growing anxiety in the flickering headlamp light.

A slow, agonizing crawl through the twisting tunnels marked the journey's continuation. Now: Once a marvel, the cave now felt like a menacing labyrinth, its vastness both refuge and trepidation. The deeper they went, the more disorienting the passages became. The constant turns and shifts in elevation created a disorienting sense of disconnection from the outside world, a feeling of being swallowed by the earth itself.

Hours passed, each one an eternity in the claustrophobic embrace of the cave. The initial fear and panic gave way to a gnawing anxiety, fueled by the dwindling supplies and the growing realization of the enormity of their situation. Rationing their water and the few energy bars they had salvaged became a ritual, every bite a minor act of defiance against the encroaching despair. The psychological impact of their isolation took its toll. Whispers and hushed conversations filled the air, the survivors sharing stories of their lives, their fears, and their hopes. The young family huddled. The elderly couple held each other close, their silence speaking volumes about the weight of their shared experience. Madison and Noah made their room together. Reassuring Madison, Noah calmed her fears.

A resourceful and comforting presence, they learned the young man's name was Ben. His calmness and strength helped to keep spirits up, a silent act of courage in the face of overwhelming adversity. He helped to organize the dwindling supplies, offering words of encouragement and reassurance, his eyes reflecting an unwavering determination that became a beacon of hope in the suffocating darkness.

As days bled into nights, marked only by the shifting shadows cast by their headlamps, the survivors experienced the claustrophobia of their predicament. The confined space, initially a refuge, now felt like a prison, its walls slowly closing in on them. The darkness, once simply an absence of light, now felt like a living entity, a heavy, oppressive blanket suffocating their spirits.

Madison continued to monitor the seismic activity, using a rudimentary seismograph she'd salvaged, interpreting the faint tremors and subterranean rumbles that resonated through the cave walls. Her findings were grim, painting a picture of a volcanic landscape in a state of absolute chaos.

The echoes of frightened voices calmed momentarily as families turned toward each other, reminding one another of their presence. Children held tight to their parents, and as Madison scanned the group, she saw Danny straightening, his determination resilient.

Hours passed as they prepared for any of the looming dangers, the cave's walls echoing their resolve. Amid the chaos of the uncertainty, Madison clung to the light of shared hope—the bonds of community unwavering even in the face of adversity.

As exhaustion set in, they rallied again, small snippets of laughter piercing through the worry as Danny and a few other children shared superhero tales among themselves, weaving stories that tangled hope with friendship.

Madison felt a warmth in her heart as she observed them, grateful for the small moments that shone brightly amid the darkness. She knew they had a long road ahead, but she was resolute: they would face it together.

"Alright, everyone!" Madison called out, moving through the cave as the children laughed and played together. "We need to gather our focus again. We're in a tough situation, and while it's good to find joy, we also need to remain vigilant."

The chatter quieted down as everyone instinctively turned their attention to her. "I want to make sure that everyone knows the plan if we have to move again. We've established our safe areas, but let's communicate the routes clearly in case we need to move swiftly."

Noah stepped up beside her, nodding. "We'll point out the exits and ensure everyone understands the safest paths. We're a united front, and we'll work together."

Families gathered again, and Madison felt the collective energy of interwoven concerns and hopes. The tight-knit assembly was a source of strength for all of them, especially the children. She approached a group of families and began explaining the routes they'd outlined.

"We'll use the left side of the cave to head to further shelter if needed. If you feel nervous or scared, please check in with one volunteer or me," she reassured them. "It's important that we stay close to one another and follow directions once we move. We'll take a headcount to make sure no one is missing.

As she moved, she could hear faint echoes from the entrance— far-off rumbles of the grounds quaking again, sending dust cascading from the walls.

"Stay close! Stay where it's solid!" Madison urged them to stay close, safely positioning families as they resumed their measured routine. The sound of distant eruptions and the vibrations became a constant reminder of the threat that loomed, but their resolve stabilized.

Despite the grim news of magma traveling around the cave system, the bit of good news is there is more flow in the tubes the magma is traveling in now. The chances of the magma going into the Jewel Cave system are low, not impossible, rather improbable. This cave system is really ideal the way it is, being mainly limestone associated with a deep aquifer and not a magma related cave system. This was a lot of geology to process, but Madison was going to explain it to Noah later. He can share that news with the group.

Noah, his ranger instincts honed over years of navigating wilderness and responding to emergencies, focused on maintaining order and morale. His experience in managing crisis situations proved invaluable, offering a sense of stability and guidance that the survivors desperately needed. He tirelessly monitored the group's physical and mental health, ensuring that everyone remained safe and calm, given the circumstances.

Chapter 10

Explosion

Everyone arrived safely in the cave. The room in the cave's mouth was very large and went back a long distance. The group followed the instructions and headed a little way in and gathered on the left side of the cave.

"Everyone, if I can have your attention for a minute. I want everyone to rummage through the bags for plastic tarps or blankets. They need to be laid out for sitting. We do not know if there are bats in the cave and if they were in this room. We don't want to catch any viruses from them," Madison announced.

Noah, as planned, also made an announcement. "I need all the men here to help me block the cave with these big rocks. We aren't looking to seal ourselves in, but we don't want all the ash coming into the cave. There is an enormous danger of breathing ash. It could kill us in a matter of minutes." All the men started gathering at the front of the cave and started moving rocks to block the front of the cave. Noah and a few other men were trying to start a fire. There were some scrap limbs in and around the mouth of the cave. The men started bringing in all the wood they could find.

Even the children were helping with carrying in the supply crates off the buses. Madison did not know what was in the crates. She knew there was food and water, but did not know how much those crates contained. What she needed to do was to make an inventory of the crates and a list of people who made it to the cave.

Madison sat down on a rock for a second, putting her face in her hands, taking a few deep breaths and was shuttering, holding back tears.

"Maddie," Noah put his hands on her shoulder to show support. "Maddie, you saved many people. No one was taking you seriously."

"Noah, everyone back there is dead. The geological board is dead. So many people died today that didn't have to. I'm not even sure we are going to survive. We are all that's left, and I'm a seismologist, not a volcanologist. There is a big difference."

"If I had to put my money on someone, it would be you every time." Noah's sharp blue eyes were piercing her down to her soul. Right then, he bent down and gave Madison a soft kiss.

"Right now, we need to explore this cave to make sure it is safe and to see if there is a water source. How long will we be stuck here?" Noah was already getting a creepy feeling about this cave.

"Ash fall can continue a few days to a few weeks. It all depends how big of an eruption there is. Also, the wind direction factors into a lot. We need to make sure there are no lava tubes connecting to this cave. My initial thought is that there is no connection; however, we are traversing roads that have been un-traveled for 700,000 years. No one believed there would be an eruption in our foreseeable futures." Madison said while brushing the sand off her pants.

"Let's go for an exploration so we can see what we are getting into." Noah said while getting two flashlights out of the bin.

They let everyone know they were going to check the cave to make sure this would be a safe spot to hold up. Only they knew if it was safe or not. This is where they were going to be until this blast was over.

Since there were a lot of earthquakes occurring, they checked the rock ceilings, and all seemed well. Nothing was loose, so the cave could handle some earthquake activity yet. There was no evidence of potential collapse. The cave was essentially dry, but there was an occasional drop of water. There was a water source somewhere in this cave system.

As they went further back, Noah was looking for evidence of an animal presence. There were no bones or scat present. There were no tracks and definitely, no animals were present.

One evening, as they sat huddled together, sharing their meager rations, the ground beneath them trembled, a violent shudder that sent a wave of panic through the group. The tremors continued, increasing in intensity, a rhythmic shaking that seemed to test the cave's structural integrity to its limits. Rocks tumbled from the ceiling, showering them with dust and debris. The survivors huddled closer; their fear was palpable in the oppressive darkness.

The cave, their sanctuary, was now a potential death trap. Relentless natural forces above and unknown dangers below trapped them, leaving their survival hanging by a thread. The fear was no longer a distant whisper; it was a monstrous roar echoing in their hearts and minds. They were facing their mortality in the cold, hard embrace of the earth. Above, the eruption continued to rage while they remained trapped in the mountain's dark heart, their future as uncertain as the rumbling ground beneath them.

Their initial panic subsided, giving way to a grim acceptance of their predicament. The cave, once a marvel of natural beauty, had become their prison, their sanctuary, and their potential tomb. Days blurred into nights, the only markers of the slow depletion of their supplies and the ever-present tremor that vibrated through the earth. Rationing became a sacred ritual, each bite of energy bar a calculated risk against the gnawing hunger. They measured their precious, dwindling water in sips.

The cave's labyrinthine passages proved a constant challenge. Navigation became a test of memory and instinct; each turn a gamble. Noah, with his years of experience navigating wilderness trails, took the lead, his headlamp cutting a path through the oppressive darkness. Madison, ever the scientist, meticulously charted their progress, marking their route on a salvaged map, her pencil scratching against the rough paper, a comforting sound in the echoing silence.

The psychological strain of confinement showed its effects. The initial fear gave way to a creeping isolation, a heavy blanket of despair that threatened to engulf them. Sleep became a fragmented luxury, punctuated by the tremors that rattled their makeshift beds of salvaged blankets and clothing. The darkness pressed in on them, amplifying the whispers of anxiety and the silent screams of fear.

But amidst the despair, a fragile camaraderie bloomed. Fear and distrust subsided, replaced by shared vulnerability against nature's relentless forces. The young family, initially withdrawn and frightened, opened up, sharing stories of their lives before the eruption, their laughter a poignant counterpoint to the grim reality. The elderly couple, their faces etched with worry, found solace in each other's presence, their hands clasped together a silent promise of mutual support.

Ben, the young athlete, emerged as a quiet leader, his innate resourcefulness a beacon of hope. Ensuring fair distribution, he helped organize their dwindling supplies. He created makeshift tools from salvaged materials, his ingenuity a constant source of admiration. He became the silent guardian, watching over the group, his calm presence a soothing balm to their anxieties.

Madison, despite her scientific stoicism, showed a surprising vulnerability. She shared her knowledge of geology, explaining the dynamics of the eruption, and her words offered a sense of understanding, even in the face of the unknown. She held quiet conversations with the children, teaching them about the wonders of the cave, transforming their fear into a sense of awe and wonder. Her unwavering determination became a source of strength for the entire group. The children enjoyed Madison's thought they were playing superheroes. It was this magical thinking that made the children happy and accepting of the conditions in the cave.

Noah remained their steady guide. Monitoring their mental and physical well-being, he offered words of encouragement and reassurance. He used his storytelling skills to distract them from their anxieties, sharing tales of his adventures in the wilderness, his voice a soothing counterpoint to the relentless tremors. He orchestrated their daily routines, creating a semblance of normalcy in their abnormal existence.

The challenges were relentless. A rockslide blocked their path, forcing a perilous journey through narrow, treacherous passages to find an alternate route. Their search for a hidden spring, prompted by water shortage, led to a discovery that quenched their thirst and deepened their awe of the cave's hidden depths. A minor injury required quick thinking and improvisation, their collaborative efforts and testing of their growing bond.

Their days revolved around the rhythm of their survival. They explored every crevice, every tunnel, searching for a more secure refuge, a less precarious position. The constant tremor added another layer of anxiety, the rumbling a constant reminder of the instability of their situation. They adapted their strategies, learned from their mistakes, and reinforced their teamwork.

Hushed conversations and shared stories filled the nights; the faint glow of their headlamps illuminated their faces, their expressions mirroring exhaustion, fear, and a flickering ember of hope. They shared their memories, their dreams, their regrets, their fears, and their hopes, and through this sharing, they forged an unbreakable bond, a testament to the human spirit's capacity for resilience and camaraderie. The cave, once a cold, indifferent landscape, became their shared home, their mutual shelter, a space that nurtured an unexpected community forged in the crucible of shared adversity. Each day was a struggle, a battle against hunger, thirst, fear, and despair. But each day also saw their resilience grow, their camaraderie deepen, and their hope flicker a little brighter in the suffocating darkness. The rumbling continued, a constant reminder of the volcano's rage, but within the dark heart of the mountain, a different life, a different strength, was slowly, steadily growing.

Chapter 11

Super Eruption

The earth shuddered, not with the familiar tremor that had become their constant companion but with a convulsive heave that ripped through the very fabric of the mountain. A low, guttural roar, like the enraged bellow of a primordial beast, erupted from the depths, a sound that resonated deep within their bones, shaking them to their core. The air itself seemed to vibrate, a palpable wave of energy that preceded the unimaginable spectacle about to unfold.

Then the mountain exploded.

Not with a single, focused blast, but with a cataclysmic, multi-pronged assault of fire, rock, and ash. The ground beneath them buckled and fractured, throwing them off balance. A blinding flash seared their eyes, even though the darkness of the cave followed by a deafening roar that surpassed even the most powerful thunderstorm they had ever experienced. It was the sound of creation itself being torn asunder, a primal scream that echoed across continents.

The cave, their refuge, their sanctuary, shuddered violently. Rocks tumbled from the ceiling, raining down on their makeshift shelters. A choking cloud of hot, abrasive ash filled the air, replacing the still, heavy scent of damp earth and minerals. The gritty, suffocating ash filled their mouths and nostrils. The stench was acrid, a sulfurous blend of burning rock and volcanic gases, a smell that seared their lungs and brought tears to their eyes.

Through cracks in the cave walls, they witnessed the eruption's terrifying display. A colossal plume of ash, black as night and impossibly vast, billowed into the sky, blotting out the sun and plunging the world into an eerie twilight. It climbed higher and higher, a monstrous, ever-growing column that dwarfed even the highest mountain peaks. Pyroclastic flows, rivers of incandescent rock and gas, cascaded down the mountain's slopes, incandescent rivers of destruction consuming everything in their path. The earth itself seemed to melt; its surface transformed into a sea of fire.

The heat intensified, a relentless wave that baked their skin and singed their hair. The air became unbearably thick and difficult to breathe, each labored inhalation a painful struggle against the suffocating ash. Panic threatened to overwhelm them, the primal fear of annihilation clawing at their minds. Noah, his ranger experience kicking in, quickly ordered them to huddle together, seeking whatever meager protection the cave walls could offer. Madison, her scientific training overriding her fears, began monitoring the air quality using salvaged equipment, her face illuminated by the faint glow of her headlamp, her eyes reflecting the chaos outside.

The tremors grew more frequent and more violent, each one a jarring reminder of the catastrophic forces at play. With groans and strains, the cave; a section of the ceiling collapsed, sending a shower of debris raining down on them. They huddled closer, their bodies pressed together, finding comfort and strength in their shared vulnerability. The children cried, their fear palpable, while the elderly couple clung to each other, the silent prayers echoing the unspoken anxieties of everyone in the group. Ben, ever resourceful, worked tirelessly, shoring up the remaining structure, creating a more secure, if still precarious, haven.

The ash continued to fall, a relentless barrage that blanketed everything in a thick gray shroud. It coated their skin, their clothes, and their hair, seeping into their lungs and causing a burning sensation in their throats. The thick gray shroud reduced visibility to almost nothing, blurring the outside world into an indistinct silhouette. The air grew thick and heavy with ash and volcanic gases, making breathing increasing difficult. They coughed, choked, and struggled for air, their eyes burning and watering.

The eruption sounded deafening; a terrifying and awe-inspiring symphony of destruction. Constant trembling shook the earth; the heat was intense and relentless, a palpable wave that radiated from the mountain. They felt like insects trapped beneath the weight of a collapsing world.

Hours bled into days. The eruption's seemingly inexhaustible fury continued. Darkness deepened, shrouding the world outside their cave in an impenetrable ash curtain. The air remained heavy and difficult to breathe, the constant coughing and choking a testament to the relentless onslaught. Their small refuge, once a marvel of nature, was now a suffocating tomb, their only hope hanging precariously on the tenuous threat of their collective will.

Despite the grim conditions, their camaraderie remained intact. They shared the remaining supplies; each morsel was a precious gift, each sip of water a moment of reprieve. They comforted each other, offering words of encouragement and support. They shared stories, memories, hopes and fears, using their combined experiences to create a small island of light in the suffocating darkness. Their collective strength, born from shared adversity, became their greatest weapon against the despair that threatened to engulf them.

Noah's storytelling skills continued to provide a much-needed distraction, his voice a comforting counterpoint to the relentless chaos outside. Madison, though offering little in terms of immediate escape, provided a framework for understanding the scale of the catastrophe, helping them to process the overwhelming sensory input and maintain a sense of hope. The only thing helping Madison get through this tough time is her time she spends alone with Noah in their little section of a cave. To have some peace, they moved their little tent to the next cave room, from where everyone else was sleeping. Ben's resourcefulness and organizational skills proved invaluable, helping them to manage their dwindling resources and maintain a sense of order amidst the turmoil. Madison's quiet strength and unwavering determination served as a beacon of hope, inspiring them to persevere, even when all seemed lost.

The eruption, while a relentless demonstration of nature's raw power, unexpectedly highlighted the resilience and adaptability of the human spirit. In the heart of that suffocating, ash-filled darkness, a different life was taking root – a community forged in the crucible of shared catastrophe. Their existence was precarious, their future uncertain, but their shared experience, their intertwined fates, bound them together, creating a powerful synergy that even the fury of a super volcano couldn't extinguish. The rumbling continued, a constant, ominous reminder of the ongoing cataclysm, but within the dark heart of the mountain, a tenacious ember of hope continued to glow, fueled by their shared courage, their unwavering determination, and their unbreakable bond. Their survival was a testament to the enduring power of the human spirit – a fragile flame in the face of unimaginable destruction.

Their journey was far from over, but for now, they clung to the present, their lives tethered to each other, their future entwined with the fate of the sleeping giant that had unleashed its fury upon the world.

The initial roar was a physical assault, a wave of sound that slammed into them, vibrating through the very bones in their bodies. It was not just loud; it was a visceral experience, a feeling of immense pressure pushing against their eardrums, a primal tremor that resonated deep within their chests. Then came the shaking – a violent, chaotic dance of the earth, a relentless shuddering that threatened to tear the cave system apart. The ground beneath them bucked and heaved, tossing them around like rag dolls in a relentless, terrifying game. Rocks, loosened by the tremors, rained down from the ceiling, a constant threat of further cave – ins. The air, thick with ash, became a suffocating blanket, each breath a struggle, each cough a painful reminder of their precarious situation.

More than just visual obscuration, the ash itself was abrasive, scratching their skin, clogging their nostrils, and filling their mouths with a gritty, acrid taste. It coated everything – their clothes, their hair, their skin – creating a suffocating, gray world.

Burning their lungs with each desperate gasp, the fine particles triggered relentless coughing fits that stole their breath. The darkness, previously a comforting shroud, was now a menacing presence, amplifying the claustrophobia and uncertainty. The faint glow of Madison's headlamp barely penetrated their suffocating cloud, casting long, eerie shadows that danced on the cave walls.

Panic threatened to overwhelm them. The children cried, their walls echoing the primal fear that gnawed at the adults. The elderly couple, their faces etched with worry, clung to each other, their silent prayers a testament to their desperation. Even Noah, the usually unflappable park ranger, felt a surge of fear. His calm demeanor, however, served as a stabilizing force, his voice a reassuring presence amidst the chaos. He barked out orders directing them to reinforce the remaining sections of the cave ceiling, using whatever makeshift tools they could find – broken branches, loose rocks, even their own backpacks. Ben, ever practical, tirelessly worked alongside him, his strength and ingenuity proving invaluable in their desperate struggle for survival.

Madison, despite her own fear, remained focused, her scientific training overriding her primal instincts. She meticulously monitored the air quality, her headlamp illuminating her determined face as she studied the readings on her salvaged equipment. Her calm demeanor and her methodical approach to the crisis were a beacon of hope for the others, reminding them that even in this desperate situation, there was still a need for rational thought and action. She meticulously documented their situation, her notes a testament to their shared struggle and a potential lifetime for rescues efforts. Her findings, though grim, provided a framework for understanding their predicament, enabling them to make informed decisions about their limited resources and the dwindling hope of rescue.

The tremors continued with their intensity; the intensity fluctuated but never truly ceasing. Each shudder sent shivers down their spines, a constant reminder of the unstable ground beneath their feet. The cave groaned under immense pressure; the rocks shifting and groaning, the air thick with the ominous sounds of the mountain's internal struggle. They listened, tense and alert to the subtle changes in the soundscape – the groaning of the earth, the creaking of the cave walls, the rumble of the shifting rocks. Each subtle shift was a start reminder of their vulnerability. They had found refuge in the cave, but it was a fragile sanctuary, always on the brink of collapse.

As days blurred into nights, the air within the cave grew heavy, a suffocating blend of ash, volcanic gases, and the stale breath of the huddled survivors. The constant coughing fits and labored breathing became a dull, monotonous rhythm, an unsettling soundtrack to their existence. Their eyes burned, their throats ached, and their bodies ached from the constant tremors and the cramped quarters. Despite the physical discomfort, however, their spirits, surprisingly, remained strong. Their camaraderie, forged in the crucible of shared adversity, proved to be a powerful weapon against despair. With all the shaking and floor buckling, the underground river and stream must have shifted and now running through a chamber they cannot find. That meant a loss of water and fish. Luckily, they saved up water, but it would not last long.

They rationed their remaining supplies, each bit of food a precious gift, each drop of water a life-giving elixir. They shared stories, memories, hopes, and fears, using their combined experiences to create a small island of light in the suffocating darkness. Noah's storytelling skills, honed over years of guiding adventures, became a crucial element in their survival. His tales of resilience, adventure, and overcoming seemingly insurmountable odds filled the cave with a much-needed sense of optimism, a powerful antidote to the despair that constantly threatened to engulf them. His stories instilled hope, reminding them of the strength of the human spirit and its extraordinary capacity for endurance. Madison's scientific expertise, though initially focused on monitoring the air quality, broadened to encompass other aspects of their survival. She analyzed their remaining resources, devising strategies for conservation and efficient allocation. She meticulously tracked the tremors, attempting to identify any patterns that might show changes in the mountain's activity. Her insights, through offering little in the way of imminent escape, provided a sense of control in an otherwise uncontrollable situation, enabling them to feel more prepared for the challenges that lay ahead. Her calm, rational approach proofed invaluable in maintaining their morale.

Ben continued his work, shoring up the cave, using every available resource to make their shelter more secure. He scavenged for materials, reinforcing the weakened structures, devising strategies for managing their waste, and conserving their limited water supplies. His tireless efforts, his quiet efficiency, and his unwavering determination provided a crucial source of support forthe group. His practical skills provided a crucial counterpoint to the theoretical expertise of Madison and the inspirational storytelling of Noah, creating a perfect blend of leadership and practical skills that enabled the group to navigate their difficult circumstances.

Relentless tremors, coughing fits, and labored breathing defined each day. The children, initially terrified, adapted, their youthful resilience a testament to the adaptability of the human spirit. The elderly couple, their initial fear gradually replaced by a quiet acceptance, found solace in each other's company, their shared experiences created a resilience that transcended the individual struggles, and their collective strength, forged in the crucible of shared adversity, became their greatest weapon against overwhelming despair. They were such a beautiful couple. Being together is all they wanted. Outside their tent, they sat, completely absorbed in each other, oblivious to everything else.

Between tremors, shared breaths replaced the silence, rustling clothes, quiet murmurs, and the comforting rhythm of shared existence. Their shared experience, their intertwined fates, bound them together, creating a powerful synergy that even the fury of a super volcano couldn't extinguish. The rumbling continued, a constant, ominous reminder of the ongoing cataclysm, but within the dark heart of the mountain, a tenacious ember of hope continued to glow, fueled by their shared courage, their unwavering determination, and their unbreakable bond.

The crackle of static, followed by a burst of distorted voice, jolted them from the oppressive silence of the cave. It was Ben, his face illuminated by the faint, ethereal glow of a salvaged radio, his expression a mixture of disbelief and horror. He'd picked up a faint signal, a ghostly whisper from the outside world, a world they had believed to be so distant yet now felt terrifyingly close.

The news was fragmented, with snippets of conversations and emergency broadcasts, choked with static and punctuated by screams. It painted a picture of unimaginable devastation. Cities shrouded in ash, communication networks collapsing, and infrastructure crumbling. Reports showed widespread panic, looting, and violent clashes over dwindling resources. The eruption, initially confined to their immediate surroundings, revealed itself to be a global catastrophe, a cataclysmic event reshaping the world.

Initial reports of the ash cloud revealed its previously unknown colossal scale. It was no longer just a local phenomenon, obscuring the sun over their valley. It was a planetary shroud, a thick blanket of darkness spreading across continents, blotting out the sun, plunging entire regions into perpetual twilight. The atmospheric disruption was causing extreme weather patterns – torrential rains in some areas as prolonged droughts in others, creating a cascade of secondary disasters. The initial earthquake that preceded the eruption had been a precursor to a global seismic shift, triggering massive aftershocks across the globe and further devastating already fragile infrastructure.

Reports detailed the societal collapse. Governments, once symbols of order and stability, were struggling to maintain control amid the chaos. Essential services – water, electricity, food supplies – were falling in many places. Law and order had broken down in various regions, replaced by a primal struggle for survival. Stories emerged of desperate people fighting over food and water, communities fractured by fear and desperation.

One particularly disturbing report detailed the complete breakdown of supply chains. Billions faced famine and disease as the once complex and interconnected global economy unraveled.

The volcanic ash, blanketing vast agricultural lands, had destroyed crops, resulting in widespread starvation and food shortages. The oceans, too, were affected, the ashfall contaminating water sources and disrupting delicate marine ecosystems.

Madison, her pale face even more drawn, translated the fragmented information, her scientific mind trying to piece together the global puzzle. She spoke of the potential for a "volcanic winter," a prolonged period of cold and darkness caused by the ash cloud blocking sunlight. The consequences of such a phenomenon, she explained, were potentially catastrophic – widespread crop failure, mass starvation, and even the extinction of certain species. Her words hung in the air, heavy with the weight of their implications.

The children, who had initially been oblivious to the true scale of the disaster, cried, their whimpers echoing the deeper anxieties of the adults. Mr. and Mrs. Henderson, their faces etched with lines of worry deeper than those carved by time, held each other tightly. Noah, his stoic demeanor crumbling under the weight of the news, stared into the distance, his eyes filled with a mixture of fear and despair. Even Ben, always the optimist, seemed subdued, the radio clutched in his hands like a lifeline that offered only grim realities.

The news brought with it a chilling sense of isolation, a realization of their profound loneliness. The world outside, once a source of comfort and connection, had become a symbol of chaos and despair. They were not just struggling for survival in a divested landscape, but they were also adrift in a world teetering on the brink of collapse. The whispers from the outside world were not just reports; they were the death knells of civilization.

The realization of their isolation was a bitter pill to swallow. Their initial hope of rescue, however fragile, now seemed utterly impossible. The communication networks were down, transportation routes obliterated, and the world outside was a terrifying maelstrom of chaos and despair. They were completely alone on a tiny island of survival in a sea of devastation.

The knowledge of the global scale of the disaster magnified the gravity of their situation a thousandfold.

This new reality weighed heavily upon them, far exceeding the weight of the ash that clogged their lungs and covered their bodies. Initially: Compared to the larger picture, the initial struggle for food and water now seemed a trivial detail in a world spiraling into chaos and a desperate fight for survival. The psychological impact was devastating; the shared trauma deepened, creating a new, deeper layer of fear and uncertainty.

They sat in silence for a long time, the static from the broken radio a constant reminder of their severed connection to the world. The silence, however, was not empty. Their shared destiny, and their interconnectedness not just as a group but as part of a global community facing the same daunting challenge, filled the silence. They universally felt their vulnerability.

Chapter 12

Deep in the Cave

ays turned into weeks, marked only by the changing light filtering through the ash cloud and the rhythm of their dwindling supplies. The radio remained their tenuous link to the outside, offering only glimpses of chaos and suffering. Each fragmentary transmission served as a grim reminder of the vastness of the destruction, a stark contrast to the claustrophobic confines of their cave. The struggles within the group intensified; the shared burden of their survival was now layered with the knowledge of the catastrophic global situation.

Madison continued her meticulous analysis, studying the ashfall patterns with renewed urgency. The knowledge that the entire planet faced a similar crisis didn't lessen the immediacy of their needs, but it gave their struggle a new meaning; their survival was not just a matter of personal resilience, but a small beacon of hope in a world shrouded in darkness.

Despite the grim reality of their circumstances, all was not bad. Whenever the children were happy, so were the parents and the group. To make the children happy, Madison and Noah would take the children exploring throughout the caves, searching for mushrooms, fish, water, and anything that could help the group. While they were exploring, they taught the children about the different shapes that were noted in the caves, understanding the underground rivers. Since this was all science, mathematics went along with the learning too. It was clear the children missed school; they were excited to receive homework and learn things they wouldn't have learned in school.

A spark of defiance persisted within the group, both children and adults alike. Their initial fear had given way to a grim determination. Their survival forged their bond, not only in the eruption's fire but also in their shared knowledge of the global catastrophe. They were part of a human race struggling against overwhelming odds. While their local struggles remained immediate and paramount, their determination now contained within it the hopes of a larger, struggling world. The whispers from the outside world were a testament to their shared fate, a stark reminder of the fragility of civilization and the resilient strength of the human spirit facing global annihilation. Their fight was not just for themselves; it was for the faint embers of hope flickering in the ashes of a world consumed by disaster.

This time that was spent in the cave slowly developed into a time with a rhythm and schedule that just so occurred naturally. The ash, a constant companion, infiltrated every crevice, coating everything in a fine gray dust. Breathing was difficult. Their eyes, perpetually gritty and sore, ached from the constant particulate matter. Yet, amidst the grime and despair, a stubborn spark of resilience flickered.

Madison, fueled by a relentless scientific curiosity, became obsessed with the ash itself. She meticulously collected samples, analyzing their composition, seeking clues that might offer a glimmer of hope, a strategy for survival. Her meticulous work uncovered something unexpected – traces of rare minerals within the volcanic ash, minerals that possessed valuable properties. This discovery, although a minor victory in the face of such immense devastation`, ignited a spark of hope within the group.

It wasn't just about survival anymore' it was about resourcefulness, about harnessing the very substance that had nearly destroyed them. She theorized about extracting these minerals, potentially using them to create rudimentary tools or even a more efficient water filtration system. Her findings, presented with her characteristic calm and precision, sparked a renewed sense of purpose within the group. Quiet slowly replaced the grim acceptance of their fate, determined hope.

Ben took Madison's findings and ran with them. He possessed an innate knack for engineering, a talent honed through years of tinkering and experimentation. He added to their limited supplies, adapting and repurposing old tools and creating makeshift equipment to begin the mineral extraction process. His dedication, fueled by a mix of survival instinct and genuine scientific interest, was infectious, inspiring the others to contribute their unique skills.

Mr. and Mrs. Henderson, despite their advanced age, surprised everyone with their unexpected strength. Their deep knowledge of herbal remedies and foraging techniques stemmed from years spent living off the land. They identified edible plants growing amidst the ash, plants that most would have dismissed as inedible. They located and carefully harvested these resilient florae, providing a crucial supplement to their dwindling food supplies. Their contribution was not just sustenance but a testament to the enduring strength of experience and knowledge.

Noah found a new purpose in maintaining the cave's structural integrity. The tremors, though less frequent now, were still a constant threat. He used his strength and engineering intuition to reinforce the cave walls, ensuring their safety. This act of physical exertion, coupled with the sense of responsibility it engendered, helped him process his grief and find a sense of purpose in their shared struggle.

The children, initially traumatized by the eruption and the grim news from the radio, adjusted to their new environment. Their youthful resilience and boundless curiosity shone through the darkness. They helped with simple tasks, learning to sort the ash samples, assisting with the filtering of water, and becoming adept at identifying edible plants. Their laughter, though often muted and tinged with sadness, was a welcome sound in the otherwise bleak environment. Their presence offered a powerful reminder that life, even it its most fragile form, was worth preserving.

The cave, initially a refuge from the eruption, became their microcosm of civilization, a testament to the enduring human spirit. They established a rudimentary system of roles and responsibilities, their collaboration becoming as crucial to their survival as food and water. The quiet hum of activity replaced the oppressive silence, the shared effort replacing the fear that had initially bound them.

The constant threat of aftershocks remained, a constant reminder of the volatile world above. But their shared resilience built a buffer against these shocks, and the unity of their purpose was far stronger than any physical structure. Each tremble felt less like an existential threat and more like a test, a hurdle to overcome together. They faced these shocks with a shared sense of purpose and shared breaths, their fear now tempered by the strength of their collective will.

Their days were no longer solely about survival but also about hope. Hope blossomed as an additional water source; a spring discovered by Mr. Henderson, high in a previously inaccessible part of the cave system. This discovery was a significant victory, alleviating their water shortages and allowing for improved hygiene and sanitation, preventing waterborne diseases.

Hope sprouted with the successful extraction of minerals from the ash. Ben, using his ingenuity, crafted rudimentary tools, improving their efficiency in collecting food, processing materials, and constructing improved shelters within the cave. These small innovations, born from necessity and ingenuity, were nothing short of miracles in their bleak reality.

Hope bloomed in their ability to create. They repurposed the surrounding materials, finding beauty and utility in the wreckage of their former lives. They carved tools from bone, crafted makeshift lamps using salvaged metal and fat from their meager food stores, and weaved rudimentary clothing from plant fibers. These creations were not just functional, they were a tangible manifestation of their will to endure, a testament to the enduring human capacity for creativity and innovation. It was a slow and arduous process, but it was building, of creation, of hope.

Hope grew from their shared stories and laughter. They found comfort in sharing their memories of the world before, recounting their individual histories, and helping each other to process their trauma. They shared songs and stories, creating a vibrant tapestry of human experience, reminding themselves of who they were, of where they came from, and of what they were fighting for. Their memories, once sources of pain, now served as powerful catalysts for hope.

The radio, though mostly filled with static, occasionally offered a glimpse of a different reality. They would hear snippets of other survivors, whispered accounts of resilience, and small acts of kindness amid chaos. These fragmentary broadcasts served as a vital connection to the outside world, a reminder that they were not alone in their struggle. These moments became beacons of hope, affirming that humanity had not extinguished its spirit; its embers still flickered despite the darkness. They were not simply surviving; they were part of a larger, global struggle, a collective fight for survival, a battle against annihilation.

Their survival wasn't merely a matter of physical endurance; it was a triumph of the human spirit. It was a testament to their ability to adapt, to innovate, to connect, and to persevere in the face of unimaginable hardship. The volcanic ash, the symbol of their devastation, had unwittingly become the raw material of their resilience. The ashes of their old world were slowly being transformed into the foundations of a new one, a testament to the enduring power of the human spirit.

Chapter 13

Discoveries

The flickering beam of Ben's makeshift lamp danced across the damp cave walls, casting long, distorted shadows that writhed and pulsed like living things. The air hung heavy, thick with the scent of damp earth and something else...something indefinably ancient and unsettling. They had ventured far beyond the initial refuge, deeper into the labyrinthine heart of Jewel Cave, driven by the desperate need for more space, more resources, and a shred of hope that the cave held more than just a crammed, dusty shelter. The entire group made this journey together.

Madison meticulously documented their progress, her notebook a testament to their perilous journey. She sketched the geological formations, noting the changes in rock composition and the subtle shifts in temperature and humidity. Each observation, however insignificant, it might seem, could hold a vital clue to understanding the cave's structure, its potential resources, and perhaps a way out.

Their progress was slow and painstaking. The passage narrowed in places, forcing them to squeeze through tight fissures, their bodi3s brushing against rough, cold stone. The uneven terrain demanded caution; a misstep could send them tumbling into the abyss. Noah, his strength still a vital asset, led the way, his sturdy frame probing the darkness ahead, his hands feeling for loose rocks and hidden caves. He was acutely aware of the constant threat of cave-ins; the faint tremors are a constant reminder of the unstable ground above. Every few steps, Noah would surprise Madison with a kiss. The kisses started increasing.

Ben tested the stability of the walls and ceiling, his eyes scanning for any signs of weakness. He had fashioned a rudimentary—sounding tool from a length of the sharpened bone and a piece of scavenged metal, tapping the rock surfaces to detect hollow areas or signs of impending collapse. His vigilance was a constant reassurance, though the weight of responsibility clearly rested heavily on his shoulders.

Mr. and Mrs. Henderson, despite their age, displayed an uncanny sense of direction and spatial awareness. They seemed to possess an intuitive understanding of the cave's unseen pathways, their knowledge of natural formations surprisingly deep. They spoke in hushed tones, their voices carrying a mystical quality, speaking of legends and whispered stories of the cave passed down through generations. These tales, although tinged with superstition, gave a sense of context to their present predicament, highlighting the long history of human interaction with this hidden world.

The children, surprisingly composed, played an unexpected role. Their smaller frames allowed them to navigate the tighter passages more easily, their fresh eyes often spotting details that the adults missed. Their quiet presence brought a sense of fragile hope, contrasting the brooding darkness and palpable tension that clung to the air. They collected interesting rock samples, and their curiosity was a small bright spot in the grim surroundings. They played games to take their minds off their situation while remaining aware of their precarious position.

As they ventured deeper, a more unsettling atmosphere enveloped them. The silence, punctuated only by the drip, drip, drip of water and their own labored breathing, pressed in on them, amplifying the sense of isolation and vulnerability. Darkness that seemed to seep into their very bones, a cold, suffocating blanket.

They encountered several side passages, some too narrow to explore, others leading to dead ends or small, damp chambers. One such chamber yielded a small pool of clear, fresh water, a welcome discovery. Mr. Henderson identified a type of moss growing near the pool, a moss traditionally used for medicinal purposes, offering potential relief for any minor injuries or illnesses.

In another passage, they stumbled upon a vast cavern far larger than their initial refuge. The sheer scale of the space was awe—inspiring, the cavern echoing with their voices and the sound of their footsteps. The cavern's ceiling arched high above them, disappearing into the inky blackness, its dimensions impossible to comprehend. A sense of wonder, mixed with trepidation, washed over them.

But the relief was short-lived. As they explored the cavern, they discovered a network of fissures crisscrossing the floor, hinting at potential instability. The ground felt strangely spongy underfoot, and there was a constant dull rumble that resonated from deep within the earth. The air felt colder, and an acrid smell, similar to sulfur, tickled their noses. This was a place that the earth itself appeared to be actively rejecting.

A disturbing discovery came as a large, almost perfectly circular opening in the cavern floor, shrouded in impenetrable darkness. The air swirling around it was noticeably colder and bore a stronger sulfurous odor. They lowered Ben's makeshift lamp into the abyss, but the beam failed to penetrate the darkness beyond a few feet. The chilling silence emanating from the chasm suggested a depth beyond their comprehension.

A heated debate ensured. Madison's scientific curiosity tempted her to explore the abyss, but Ben, prioritizing practicality over scientific discovery, strongly advised against it. The potential danger was too great, and the risk of a cave-in or some unknown hazard was far too significant. After considerable discussion, fraught with tension and anxiety, they reluctantly agreed to leave the abyss unexplored, at least for now.

Their continued exploration revealed more chambers, some containing small deposits of minerals – the same minerals Madison had discovered in the volcanic ash, only in purer, more concentrated forms. This discovery was a significant victory, offering the potential for creating tools and equipment far superior to those they had fashioned from the ash. This unexpected wealth buoyed their spirits.

As they moved deeper into the labyrinth, they uncovered signs of previous inhabitants: faint markings on the walls, crude tools long abandoned, hinting at a long-forgotten civilization that had once dwelled in this subterranean world. These remnants, uncovered amidst the darkness, brought to life a history that had been silent for centuries.

The journey had been fraught with perils, both physical and psychological. The constant threat of cave-ins, the claustrophobia of the narrow passages, the echoing silence of the vast caverns, and the ever-present uncertainty had tested the group's resolve. But they had persevered, their collective resilience bolstered by their shared determination to overcome their adversity. Their exploration of Jewel Cave, though far from over, had yielded vital resources and a renewed sense of hope. They had found a larger, more habitable space, a refuge against the harsh world above, and an unforeseen richness hidden beneath the earth's surface. The journey had been arduous, but the rewards were undeniable, reminding them that even in the darkest depths, life finds a way. And for this group, survival meant more than just enduring; it was about finding a new beginning, a new hope, in the unlikeliest of places.

As the reality of their limited resources sunk in, the initial euphoria of finding the larger cavern quickly faded. The small pool of water, while a blessing, was hardly enough to sustain ten people indefinitely. The meager supply of moss, while potentially medicinal, offered no sustenance. Their initial stock of food, already dwindling, now seemed pathetically inadequate. They painstakingly conserved the precious few energy bars and dehydrated meals, rationing them with agonizing precision; each bite was a calculated decision that weighed heavily on their stomachs and minds.

A thick tension now hung in the air, replacing the atmosphere of hopeful discovery. Hushed arguments replaced the vibrant discussions about geological formations and ancient civilizations over the last remaining can of peaches. The children, initially resilient, showed signs of fatigue and hunger. Their games became quieter, their laughter less frequent, replaced by a weary silence that mirrored the anxieties of the adults.

Ben took charge of rationing. He meticulously measured out each portion, ensuring an equal distribution, but even his fairness couldn't quell the growing discontent. Madison battled gnawing hunger pangs that dulled her sharp intellect. Her usually meticulous notes were becoming scribbled and rushed, a reflection of her depleted energy. Her hunger seemed to affect even her observations.

Noah weakened. He tried giving Madison some of his food every meal, but she refused to take it. The constant physical exertion, compounded by the lack of proper nutrition, was taking its toll. His usually sturdy frame appeared gaunter, his movements slower, less confident. He snapped at minor irritations, his patience wearing thin. The usually cheerful strength of his character faltered as hunger chipped away at his resolve. Impatience and irritability replaced his quiet strength. Everyone was irritable now.

Mr. and Mrs. Henderson, though seemingly unfazed by the hardships, bore the weight of the situation with quiet dignity. Their knowledge of herbs and medicinal plants, while comforting in theory, offered little practical solace in their present predicament. Their whispered stories, once a source of comfort, now seemed to carry a note of foreboding reflecting the growing despair. The tales of survival from previous inhabitants felt less like inspirational stories and more like grim warnings.

The scarcity of resources exacerbated existing tensions. Madison advocated for exploring the mysterious abyss, arguing that it might hold vital resources – water, food, or a way out. Ben, however, remained steadfast in his opposition. He prioritized safety, believing the risks involved outweighed any potential rewards. Their arguments became increasingly heated, their differences amplified by their hunger and exhaustion.

The limited supplies also fueled a simmering conflict between Ben and Noah. While Ben prioritized strict rationing, Noah, driven by instinct and primal need, argued for a more flexible approach. He believed they needed to conserve their energy, and depleting their supplies too slowly could be just as disastrous as depleting them too quickly. He suggested prioritizing those capable of contributing most to their survival, a proposition that both angered and frightened Madison.

Their hunger affected not just their physical strength but their mental resilience. Paranoia and suspicion crept into their interactions. Whispers of betrayal and hoarding replaced once open dialogue. People easily leveled accusations, however unfounded, and fiercely defended them. The close-knit camaraderie of their earlier journey seemed to dissolve, the bonds of trust frayed by the gnawing pressure of starvation.

Even the children were not immune to the deteriorating mental state of the adults. The constant bickering, the tension-filled silences, and the palpable sense of despair cast a shadow over their youthful innocence. Anxious fidgeting and tearful outbursts, mirroring the growing unrest amongst the adults, replaced their quiet play. One-night, young Lily woke screaming after a nightmare involving starvation, a silent testimony to the psychological toll that the situation had taken.

What was initially a source of hope, the discovery of the mineral deposits, now felt cruel. The valuable minerals seemed almost mocking in their abundance, useless without the proper tools and energy to extract and process them. The glittering crystals, reflecting the faint light of Ben's lamp, seemed to amplify the darkness of their situation.

One evening, a heated argument erupted between Ben and Madison. The argument over the remaining energy bars escalated, fueled by exhaustion, hunger, and the constant pressure of their desperate situation. It ended with the shattering of a precious ceramic canteen, an act of impulsive fury that served as a stark symbol of their collective despair.

Guilt and regret filled the heavy silence that followed. Huddled in the darkness, the group felt the heavy weight of their predicament. Their depleted resources had weakened them physically and fractured the foundation of their group dynamic. The scarcity had transformed a once-unified team into a collection of anxious, hungry individuals struggling to maintain their sanity. Their refuge had become a prison; the cave's darkness mirroring the despair threatening to consume them.

Relentlessly, the constant dripping of water underscored their dwindling supplies, breaking the silence and countering their failing hope. The air hung heavy knowing that their survival depended not only on finding more resources. Rebuilding the trust and unity that the relentless pressure of scarcity had shattered, their fight for survival had reached a new, perilous stage. A battle against not just the harsh elements of the cave, but against the corrosive effects of hunger and despair on their shared humanity. The darkness held more than just the physical threats of the cave; it held the threat of internal collapse. They had to navigate the darkness not just physically but emotionally if they hoped to find a path to freedom.

The rhythmic drip, drip, drip of water echoed in the oppressive silence, a morbid metronome marking the passage of time and the dwindling of their hope. Then, a faint sound, almost imperceptible at first, cut through the oppressive quiet – a low gurgle, like water moving over smooth stones. It came from a direction they hadn't explored, a passage they hadn't even noticed during their initial frantic search.

Madison was the first to identify the source. "There's something there," she whispered, her voice barely audible above the ceaseless dripping. Her usually sharp gaze, dulled by hunger and exhaustion, now held a flicker of renewed determination. The sound had pierced through the veil of despair, reigniting a spark of hope in her weary heart.

Cautiously, Ben approached the narrow passage, his lamp beam cutting through the inky blackness. The air, noticeably cooler and damper here, carried an unfamiliar scent – a faint earthy smell, tinged with the metallic tang of minerals and something else...something strangely organic. He motioned for Noah to join him, their movements deliberate, careful, each step a testament to their heightened awareness.

A larger chamber, far bigger than any they had previously explored, opened up beyond the passage. The air hung heavy with moisture; the silence broken only by the gentle lapping of water against unseen shores. And then, they saw it: a subterranean lake, its surface reflecting the weak light from their lamps, its depths veiled in an impenetrable darkness. The water, unlike the stagnant pool in their original cavern, was crystal clear, its surface undisturbed except for the occasional ripple that hinted at unseen currents.

The sheer scale of the lake was breathtaking. It extended as far as the eye could see, the walls of the cavern rising high above, disappearing into the shadows. The discovery sparked a wave of elation that momentarily eclipsed their hunger and exhaustion. It was a monumental find, a potential lifeline in this subterranean labyrinth. The lake offered the promise of fresh water; perhaps even a means of escape, a way to navigate this underground world.

As they explored the edge of the lake, they made another discovery, equally astonishing. Embedded in the damp cave walls, partially submerged in the lake's crystal-clear waters, were intricate carvings. They weren't natural formations; these were deliberate, crafted with skill and precision. They appeared to be ancient symbols, depictions of strange creatures, and what looked like celestial bodies. The carvings darkened by time and water spoke of civilization that had existed here long before them, a civilization that had survived, and perhaps even thrive, in this hidden world.

The discovery sent a shiver down their spines, a mixture of awe and unease. It was a revelation that transcended their immediate predicament, adding another layer of mystery to the already complex puzzle of their subterranean prison. The carving was not mere decoration; they were a narrative, a silent testament to a lost culture, a story waiting to be deciphered. This historical element breathed new life into their survival narrative, transforming their desperate struggle from a mere battle for survival to a quest for understanding. Their hunger and exhaustion momentarily receded, replaced by a potent cocktail of curiosity, excitement, and a healthy dose of cautious optimism.

Exploring further, they found another chamber, this one smaller and drier, connected to the main cavern by a narrow passage. Here, nestled amongst the rocks were remnants of what appeared to be ancient dwellings – rudimentary structures made of stone and some kind of hardened clay. Scattered among the ruins were fragments of pottery, tools crafted from bone and stone, and even woven fabrics that, despite the passage of time, kept traces of intricate designs. These weren't merely scraps; they were pieces of forgotten history, relics of a people who had once called this place home.

The discovery fueled the renewed sense of purpose. To meet their immediate needs, the lake offered fresh water, fishing opportunities, and a method for crossing the cavern. The relics offered a glimpse into the past and the potential to learn from the ingenuity and resilience of a bygone civilization. They might even discover clues to help them find a way out. The sheer scale of what they'd discovered spurred a fierce wave of hope to course through their starved and weary bodies.

The children, who had initially watched the explorations with anxious eyes, their faces pale and drawn, were now mesmerized by the ancient carvings and the mysterious artifacts. Lily, her earlier nightmare forgotten, pointed excitedly at a particular carving, her eyes wide with wonder. Even the youngest, Tommy, seemed captivated by the unusual beauty of the smooth, strangely shaped stones. The discovery of this ancient world brought a sense of shared wonder, temporarily diverting their attention from the harsh realities of their situation.

The adults, too, found renewed purpose in their situation. Ben planned to access the lake's resources. He envisioned building a crude raft from fallen branches and sturdy vines, a means of exploring the lake's extent and searching for food. Madison, her scientific curiosity piqued, meticulously documented the carvings and artifacts, hoping to glean insights into the culture of the ancient inhabitants. She recognized some patterns that hinted at an advanced understanding of astronomy, possibly using the subterranean lake's reflection for astronomical observations. It was a discovery that added another layer to the complexity of their subterranean world.

Noah worked with Ben; their earlier conflict was forgotten in the face of their shared excitement. The renewed purpose reinvigorated his physical strength, though still depleted. He set about collecting sturdy materials for the raft-building project, his movement less labored, his spirit more upbeat.

Even Mr. and Mrs. Henderson, who had observed the discoveries with a solemn curiosity, offered their knowledge of herbal remedies, suggesting plants that might purify the water, ensuring its safe consumption.

The discovery of the ancient civilization, however, also brought with it a new set of challenges. The artifacts and carvings hinted at a richer, more complex history than they could have ever imagined. Questions arose about this vanished culture, their reasons for living in this hidden world, and ultimately, what happened to them. The possibilities spurred a blend of hope, excitement, and trepidation, leaving the survivors filled with a sense of wonder, and the need to learn more. The cave, no longer simply a prison, transformed into a portal to another time, a living museum awaiting explorations.

Meticulous documentation of the carvings and artifacts became an essential part of their survival strategy. Madison's detailed sketches and notes could reveal clues to help them navigate the cavern complex and perhaps even find a way to the surface. The intricate patterns, meticulously recorded, might hold a hidden map, a secret passage, or perhaps even a message from the ancient inhabitants. Although nobody was an expert in ancient civilizations, the drawings resembled Incan work. Their exploration had transformed from a desperate struggle for survival into a captivating quest for knowledge and understanding, an interesting blend of science, history, and sheer survival into a captivating quest for knowledge and understanding, an interesting blend of science, history, and sheer survival against all odds. The darkness, once a symbol of their despair, now held the promise of discovery. The survival struggle had a new, potent adversary – the allure of an ancient, lost civilization. As they explored this section of the cave, there seemed to be a loud echo when talking. As they reached the back of the cave, they Madison noticed there was a stone altar that contained small beads of different colors. She had read somewhere these beads were used to offer prayers to their God.

Madison looked carefully behind the altar; the beads and rocks were stacked upon each other, and she felt a breeze when she raised her hand. Madison started unslacking the rocks and held up her light. The room glimmered with a yellow gold glow. Gold filled the entire room!

Everyone gasped! There were many suggestions where this gold came from, but being from the west, there was always talk of Aztec gold.

There will never be a day this community has to worry about rebuilding and being secure again. Now they all had to find a way out.

Chapter 14

Creatures

The euphoria of their discovery – the subterranean lake, the ancient carvings, the remnants of a lost civilization – faded as a new, chilling reality seeped into their awareness. The cave wasn't empty. It wasn't just silent; it was listening.

A low, guttural growl, barely audible at first, broke the stillness down their spines, far more unsettling than any drip or gurgle of water. Ben shone his lamp into the shadows, his hand instinctively reaching for the makeshift spear he'd fashioned from a sharpened branch. Nothing was immediately visible, but the air itself seemed to vibrate with a palpable sense of unease.

Hours later, as they were preparing a meager meal of roasted grubs – a far cry from their previous expectations – an unfamiliar sound emerged, this one closer, sharper. A high-pitched screech, like nails scraping across stone, sent Lily scrambling into her mother's arms.

The sound echoed through the cavern, bouncing off the uneven walls and creating an unnerving symphony of fear.

Then came the sight. A creature unlike anything they had ever imagined emerged from a narrow fissure in the cave wall. It was small, no larger than a gigantic rat, but its appearance was horrifying. Its skin was translucent, almost skeletal, revealing a network of pulsating veins beneath. Its eyes, large and black, glowed with an unsettling intensity, reflecting the lamplight with an unnerving brilliance. Thin and spindly legs moved with unnatural speed and agility, propelling it gracefully across the cavern floor. It looked like a land/freshwater crab. Since they lived in isolation in a cave, this unknown creature was about to become something else – dinner.

It moved with a disturbing fluidity; its body contorting in ways that defied the laws of conventional anatomy. It seemed to melt through shadows, appearing and disappearing with a disconcerting case; making it nearly impossible to track. It darted towards a small pile of their collected firewood, snatching a twig and vanishing back into the darkness as quickly as it had appeared.

One by one they came, a wave of these unsettling creatures emerging from the shadows. Their numbers seemed endless, their movements coordinated, their intentions unclear. They were clearly scavengers, drawn to the faint scent of their fire, but their unnerving appearance and their uncanny ability to blend into the darkness created to profound sense of dread. Catching them was very easy. The group made nets out of scraps of clothes. They made hooks from bone fragments. Nobody was going to bed hungry tonight.

The initial panic gave way to a grim determination. They realized they couldn't ignore these creatures. Their presence posed a significant threat to their meager supplies of food and firewood, potentially jeopardizing their already precarious situation. Ben, demonstrating his resourcefulness, devised a series of traps using sharpened sticks and stones, strategically placing them around their makeshift camp.

Madison focused on studying the creatures, meticulously documenting their behavior and physical characteristics. Her observations revealed a surprising complexity in their actions. They seemed to communicate with each other using a series of high-pitched chirps and clicks, almost imperceptible to the human ear yet clearly understood within their own strange society. She hypothesized they had adapted to survive in the extreme conditions of the cave, with their translucent skin allowing them to absorb minimal light and their agility enabling them to navigate the labyrinthine passages with ease.

This near-catastrophe forced them to reassess their situation. The cave, once a potential haven, was now a hostile environment, teaming with unseen dangers. They understood the ancient inhabitants' carvings might depict more than a lost civilization; perhaps they also documented the dangers of the cave, the very creatures that now threatened the survivors. Their exploration became a race against time; a desperate search for a way out before the creatures, or the cave itself, overwhelmed them.

Their explorations continued, fueled by a new urgency. In the deeper parts of the cave, they discovered larger creatures lurking. They were far more terrifying, possessing powerful jaws and claws capable of inflicting serious injuries. The "crabs" seemed to be territorial, guarding specific areas of the cavern. One such encounter with one of the large, spider-like creatures nearly ended tragically for Ben, leaving him with a deep gash on his arm, a stark reminder of their vulnerability.

Madison's study of the carvings and artifacts intensified. She noticed some symbols seemed to depict the creatures, possibly warnings or descriptions of their behavior and habitats. She suspected that the ancient inhabitants had not only survived in this cave but had also developed intricate strategies to co-exist with the creatures, perhaps even understanding their complex social structures. Her detailed sketches and notes became essential survival tools, not just historical records.

The constant threat of the cave creatures forced the survivors to become more resourceful and united. They learned to cooperate, to rely on each other's strengths, to trust their instincts. Their fear turned into resilience, their despair into determination. They viewed the creatures not just as threats but as challenges, a test of their will to survive, and a measure of their understanding of this ancient, subterranean world. At least no one was hungry anymore.

The cave, once a silent, dark prison, now pulsed with life – a life that was both wondrous and terrifying. The survivors' quest for survival had grown. It was no longer just a fight against the darkness and starvation, but a battle against the creatures of the night, a dance with the unknown, a struggle for survival in the literal heart of the earth. The lake, once a symbol of hope, now served as a precarious lifeline, constantly threatened by the ever-present shadow of the creatures that shared their subterranean world. The ancient history of the cave, once a source of wonder, now held clues to their survival – if only they could decipher them before the creatures overwhelmed them. Their journey into the heart of the earth had become a terrifying blend of exploration and survival, a fight for life in a world where the dangers lurked not only in the darkness but also in the very depths of the earth itself. The very air they breathed vibrated with a constant, low hum of menace, a reminder that survival in this forgotten world was a daily struggle against the very fabric of the earth itself.

The rhythmic drip of water, a constant companion in the subterranean prison, seemed to echo the pounding of Madison's heart. For days, the relentless pressure of survival had pushed them to the brink. The creatures, those unsettling, translucent beings, had become a constant, gnawing anxiety. Sleep offered brief respite; the high-pitched chirps and clicks, a sinister lullaby, haunted their dreams. Even the relative safety of their makeshift camp felt precarious, a fragile bubble in a sea of unseen dangers. Hope, once a flickering candle, had dwindled to a faint ember.

Then, amidst the despair, a glimmer. It began with a detail almost insignificant on its own: a peculiar smoothness in the cave wall, a deviation from the rough, uneven texture that had characterized their surroundings. Ben, ever observant, noticed it while attempting to reinforce their defenses against the creatures. He touched it tentatively, his fingers tracing the anomaly. It felt strangely warm to the touch, a stark contrast to the chilling dampness of the surrounding stone.

Intrigued, Madison inspected the area. She discovered a seam, barely visible in the dim light, that seemed to run along the wall for several feet. A faint, almost imperceptible vibration emanated from it, a subtle hum that resonated deep within her chest. Her geologist's instinct, honed over years of studying the earth's hidden processes, recognized it instantly: a tremor, not the violent shaking of an earthquake, but a subtle, rhythmic pulse, showing movement deep with the rock.

Carefully and meticulously, they investigated. Using their makeshift tools – sharpened stones and branches – they chipped away at the stone, slowly revealing a narrow passage concealed behind the seemingly solid wall. The air within the passage felt different, warmer and slightly fresher, carrying a faint whiff of something akin to…earth. Not the stale, damp air of the cave but the rich, loamy scent of the surface world.

The discovery sent a wave of elation through them. The exhaustion, the fear, the gnawing despair – all seemed to melt away in the face of this renewed hope. Their eyes, dulled by days of unrelenting darkness, regained a spark of vitality. Their movements, previously sluggish and hesitant, became infused with a renewed energy, a frantic eagerness to explore.

Noah let out a whoop of joy, a sound that echoed strangely in the cavern's vast emptiness. Lily, her face alight with a mix of fear and exhilaration, clung to her mother's hand, her eyes wide with anticipation. Even Ben, the pragmatist, allowed himself a rare smile, a subtle crack in his stoic façade. For the first time in days, laughter, hesitant but genuine, filled the air.

The passage was narrow, barely wide enough for one person to squeeze through. They decided that Ben, the strongest and most agile, would go first, followed by Madison, then Noah, with Lily at last, cradled securely in her mother's arms. Ben, armed with his spear and his ever-present lamp, crawled forward cautiously, his voice echoing ahead, reassuring his family. The passage sloped gently downwards, leading them deeper into the unknown.

The air gradually became more pleasant. The rhythmic pulse intensified, accompanied by a faint, almost inaudible rushing sound, like the whisper of a distant waterfall. After what seemed like an eternity, Ben stopped, his voice a low whisper. "I see light," he announced, his words filled with a mixture of awe and disbelief.

Slowly, cautiously, he emerged into a larger cavern. The sight that greeted them was breathtaking. A vast subterranean chamber opened before them, lit by a faint, ethereal glow. A narrow shaft of light pierced the ceiling, illuminating a subterranean lake far larger than the one they had discovered earlier. The air here was noticeably warmer, and the sound of rushing water was more distant now. They could smell the earthy scent, not just faintly, but strongly now. A thin, subterranean river was flowing swiftly from beneath an underground waterfall flowing to the larger lake.

But it wasn't just the beauty that stunned them. On the far side of the chamber, partially submerged in the lake, they saw it: a structure, partially ruined but unmistakably artificial. It looked like the remains of a dock or a landing stage, made of some unknown, dark, resilient material. And on the edge of the water, partially obscured by the murky waters, glimmered something metallic – something that, at first, they only partially believed. The reflection of the shaft of light glinted on a surface, revealing, almost incredibly, what looked to be a piece of metal that resembled a...satellite dish. Partially rusted and damaged by age, but undeniably a technological artifact.

This discovery was even more profound than the existence of the lake and the carvings. It was more than just a sign of a lost civilization; it was evidence of contact with the outside world, a potential lifeline, a beacon of hope in the crushing darkness. Tears of relief and job streamed down Madison's face, a mixture of relief and disbelief. The despair and fear of the last days seemed to fade as a new and powerful emotion flooded through them – an overwhelming sense of hope.

Their journey had been a descent into darkness, a struggle for survival against the unseen horrors of the earth. But now, in the heart of this subterranean world, they had stumbled upon a potential path to escape. The ancient carvings had led them to the lake, a source of water, and a potential lifeline. But this latest discovery, the unmistakable signs of a technology far beyond their understanding, suggested something more profound: a potential connection to a world beyond the claustrophobic confines of the cave, a possible salvation from the ever-present shadow of the creatures. The darkness of the cave remained, the ever-present danger of the creatures still threatened, yet somehow, it no longer seemed so overwhelming. Their journey, once a desperate fight for survival, now felt like a thrilling race against time, a journey towards the light. The ancient cave, once a tomb, now held the key to their freedom.

Chapter 15

Survivors

The subterranean river, a lifeline in this hidden world, carried them further into the earth's embrace. The rhythmic pulse of the earth, once a subtle hum, now thrummed with palpable intensity, a constant reminder of the cataclysmic event that had reshaped their world. The faint, ethereal glow illuminating the cavern was a stark contrast to the memory of the suffocating darkness they had endured. But even in this newfound sanctuary, the weight of what they had left behind pressed heavily upon them.

Madison couldn't shake the images of devastation. The eruption hadn't just been a local catastrophe; it had been a global event, an unimaginable inferno that had swallowed cities whole, choked the skies with ash, and plunged the world into chaos. The tremors that had ravaged the planet. She pictured the ash clouds, vast and suffocating, blotting out the sun, plunging entire regions into perpetual twilight. The air, thick with ash and noxious gases, had rendered breathing a struggle, a constant battle for survival against the very elements.

The satellite dish fragment, a relic of a forgotten age, was a poignant symbol of humanity's technological prowess and its utter vulnerability in the face of nature's raw power. It was a stark reminder that even our most advanced creations were no match for the fury of a super volcano. She thought of the billions, perhaps more, who hadn't survived the initial blast. Those incinerated instantly, those who perished slowly, suffocated by the ash-filled air, starved by the failure of agriculture. A landscape scarred by fire and ash, a testament to the planet's exceptional might, replaced the world they knew.

A cascade of secondary effects, a domino effect of disaster that had rippled across the globe, had followed the initial devastation. The ash clouds had blocked sunlight, leading to a catastrophic drop in global temperatures and a volcanic winter that had frozen crops and choked life out of fertile lands. Widespread famine followed a relentless hunger that had decimated populations and plunged humanity into a desperate struggle for survival. The infrastructure that had once supported billions, the intricate networks of transportation, communication, and agriculture, had crumbled under the weight of the catastrophe. Entire societies had collapsed, replaced by a desperate scramble for resourced, a brutal fight for survival where the rules of civilization had become obsolete.

The endless worry caused by the radio silence now made chilling sense. Besides wiping out communications networks, the eruption also destroyed a significant portion of the Earth's ecosystem. The lace of sunlight had caused a near-total crop failure in many regions. The few surviving plants struggled under the darkness and poisonous ash. With this came the collapse of the food chain. People were starving, and those who survived the initial blast were now succumbing to hunger and disease.

Noah spoke of the rumors, the whispers carried on the wind from other pockets of survival. Tales of desperate bands of survivors scavenging for scraps in the ravaged landscape, battling each other for dwindling resources. Tales of lawless territories, where the strong prey on the weak, and civilization had descended into anarchy. He'd heard stories of cannibalism, a grim testament to the depths of human desperation in the face of unimaginable hunger. Even the most civilized societies couldn't withstand the pressure of widespread starvation and societal collapse. Every interaction between groups of survivors ended with violence or betrayal.

Lily seemed to grasp the enormity of the catastrophe. Her wide, innocent eyes held a depth of understanding that belied her years. Her quiet observations and her occasional pointed questions revealed a profound awareness of the fragility of life, the precarious balance between survival and extinction. She had witnessed the chaos and violence first-hand, the desperate scramble for food and water. She recalled the screams and cries of those who had succumbed to starvation or disease. The experience imprinted the memory deep into her psyche, constantly reminding her of the world's fragility.

Ben focused on the immediate challenges. He spoke of the need to find a way out, to reach the surface, to navigate the treacherous landscape that lay beyond. His concern wasn't just for his own family, but for the larger struggle for survival. He emphasized the need to rebuild, find a way to re-establish order, and salvage what remained of humanity's potential. He worried about the few remaining pockets of civilization fighting for survival amidst the ash-choked wasteland.

The discovery of the satellite dish fragment, a remnant of a bygone era of technological advancement, offered a flicker of hope, a potential lifeline in the vast ocean of despair. It was a testament to human ingenuity, a symbol of a world that once was. But it also represented the gap between the world and the stark reality of their present. The technology represented a potential breakthrough, a chance to reconnect with the outside world, access information, and potentially find other survivors. However, it also highlighted how unprepared humanity was for a disaster on this scale. The lack of preparedness and failing to expect and mitigate such an event contributed to the extent of the catastrophe.

The weight of the global devastation bore down on them, a crushing burden that threatened to extinguish the fragile ember of hope they had found. But they held on, clinging to the belief that even amidst the ashes, even in the earth's heart, a chance for survival still existed. The satellite dish, a symbol of a world lost, also represented a potential pathway to a new beginning. They had to find a way out, to reach the surface, and to face the grim realities of a world irrevocably changed. The journey ahead was uncertain, perilous, and fraught with danger. But it was a journey they had to take for themselves, for the memory of those they had lost, and for the future of humanity itself. The fight for survival was far from over. It had just begun.

The satellite dish fragment, a twisted mockery of former technological prowess, lay before them, a beacon of hope in the oppressive darkness. It was a testament to humanity's ingenuity, a symbol of connection in a world fractured beyond repair. But its condition was far from ideal. Rust consumed its once-gleaming surface, and clearly damaged the delicate internal mechanisms, perhaps beyond repair. Yet, the possibility of using it to contact the outside world remained a flickering flame I the hearts of the survivors.

Ben began the assessment. His hands, calloused from years of fieldwork, moved over the warped metal with a practiced touch. He examined the intricate network of wires and the shattered components, searching for any sign of salvageable parts. He traced the lines of the parabolic dish, calculating the extent of the damage and estimating the feasibility of restoration. His expertise, honed over years of working in satellite technology, was crucial in this desperate attempt at communication.

"The main dish itself seems structurally sound," Ben announced, his voice low and measured. "But the receiver unit…that's toast. And the power source is completely gone." He gestured towards a tangle of corroded wires, once part of a complex electrical system. "We're talking about a complete rebuild. We'd need to find components and a viable power source. Even if we did that, sending a signal through this amount of atmospheric interference would be incredibly difficult."

Madison weighed in. "The ash cloud is still incredibly thick. Even if we could restore the dish, getting a signal through to a satellite or to any other ground-based receiver is questionable. The electrical interference from the still-active geothermal activity might further complicate things. We may face insurmountable obstacles."

Noah approached the dish with cautious excitement. "But if we can't contact anyone, then we're truly alone. We need to try. We owe it to those we lost."

The task before them was monumental. Sourcing the components required venturing into the ravaged world above, a prospect fraught with danger. Scavenging for parts in a lawless wasteland was a suicide mission, a desperate gamble with their lives. Each foray into the devastated landscape carried the risk of encountering hostile survivors, desperate for resources, or falling prey to the unpredictable elements. The poisoned air, contaminated water, and the ever-present danger of collapsing infrastructure posed constant threats. Every step outside the relative safety of their subterranean sanctuary was a roll of the dice.

Beyond the immediate physical challenges, they faced a technological hurdle that was, in its own way, equally daunting. Even if they somehow located and assemble the components, the technical knowledge to reassemble and operate the satellite dish was sparse. Much of the relevant expertise had likely perished in the catastrophe.

Their collective knowledge, though extensive in its individual areas, lacked the specialized skills needed to accomplish this task. They were amateur radio operators at best, facing a problem of the kind that usually required teams of experts and state-of-the-art equipment.

Lily pointed to a section of the dish partially shielded from the elements. "Maybe this part is still usable," she suggested, her small finger tracing a less-corroded area. It was a slight detail, a minor point of hope, but it was enough to reignite their determination.

The weeks that followed were a blur of frantic activity. Their subterranean haven, once a sanctuary, transformed into a makeshift workshop. They searched the cavern for anything they could repurpose – wires, metal scraps, even fragments of rock crystal, hoping to find materials that could replace missing components. They worked tirelessly, driven by a mixture of hope and desperation, their determination fueled by the faint possibility of a connection with the outside world.

Ben, with Noah's help, painstakingly disassembled and reassembled parts of the dish, often working by the faint ethereal glow emanating from the geothermal vents. Madison used her geological knowledge to locate potential sources of energy – geothermal vents and decaying organic matter that might provide a source of fuel. Lily proved invaluable in the meticulous work of repairing the delicate internal mechanisms.

Their efforts were not without setbacks. They faced equipment failures, damaged components, and overwhelming frustration. There were moments of doubt when the sheer scale of the task felt insurmountable, when the weight of their situation threatened to crush their spirits. But they persevered, clinging to the hope that their efforts would not be in vain.

Finally, after weeks of relentless work, they had assembled a makeshift power source using a combination of geothermal energy and scavenged batteries. They had cobbled together a functional receiver, using salvaged parts, and Lily's surprisingly deft handiwork. The repaired satellite dish, while a far cry from its former glory, was now, at least, capable of transmitting a signal.

The moment of truth arrived under a sky perpetually veiled in ash-laden twilight. They aimed the makeshift dish toward the heavens, their hearts pounding with a mixture of hope and apprehension. Ben carefully adjusted the frequency, his fingers dancing over the makeshift controls. The silence stretched on; an eternity measured in heartbeats before a faint crackle echoed from the receiver. A surge of electricity ran through them, a wave of collective exhilaration that momentarily eclipsed their despair.

They had established contact. The signal was faint, distorted, barely audible, but it was there – a testament to their resilience, to the indomitable human spirit. It was a minor victory, a fleeting moment of hope in a world consumed by darkness. But it was enough to fuel their determination, to renew their belief in the possibility of survival, and to continue their desperate fight to rebuild a world shattered beyond recognition. The long shadow of the eruption still loomed, but now they had a glimmer of light to guide them through the darkness. The journey was far from over, but for the first time since the catastrophe, they were not completely alone.

Chapter 16

Baby Steps

The crackle of static, initially a source of immense relief, soon morphed into something more complex, more intriguing. It wasn't just random noise; there were patterns and rhythmic pulses that hinted at a structured signal. Ben crudely assembled an oscilloscope, adjusted the frequency, painstakingly fine-tuning the receiver. The static lessened, revealing a faint, distorted voice, almost swallowed by the omnipresent hiss of atmospheric interference. It was a woman's voice, strained and weak but undeniably human.

A collective gasp echoed through their makeshift workshop. Hope, previously a fragile ember, flared into a brilliant flame. They weren't alone. The eruption, the devastation, the seemingly endless despair – it hadn't erased humanity entirely. There were others, somewhere out there, clinging to life just as they were.

The signal was too weak to decipher words clearly. It was a series of fragmented sounds, punctuated by bursts of static, yet the cadence, the rhythm of the transmission, suggested a deliberate attempt at communication. Lily, surprisingly fluent in several forms of Morse code, leaned forward, her brow furrowed in concentration. "It's…it's Morse Code, she whispered, her voice barely audible above the hum of their makeshift power source.

For hours, they worked tirelessly, meticulously decoding the fragmented signals. Ben meticulously documented each pulse, each pause, and each flicker of sound on a makeshift notepad while Lily translated the series of dots and dashes into letters and words. Madison monitored the signal strength, looking for patterns in the interference that might reveal the location of the transmitter. Noah tirelessly tweaked the antennae, constantly searching for a stronger signal, his youthful energy a counterpoint to the intense focus of the others.

The message, when finally pieced together, was brief, almost cryptic: "…isolated…southwest…seeking…others…" It was a desperate plea, a cry for help to echo across the desolate landscape. The coordinates, though incomplete, provided a general direction – southwest, a vast, uncharted territory beyond their immediate surroundings.

Their established routine fractured as the discovery sent shockwaves through their small group. A far larger, more complex challenge suddenly overshadowed the immediate task of survival, of securing food and shelter: reaching out to these other survivors. The implications were enormous, stirring a potent mix of hope and apprehension within each of them.

Ben was the first to voice his concerns. "Southwest," he muttered, tracing the direction on their rudimentary map. "That's a significant distance, and we know nothing about the terrain. It could be dangerous, even impassable." He outlined the risks:

collapsing infrastructure, hostile scavengers, poisonous air, and the ever-present threat of unpredictable elements.

Madison pointed out, "A weak signal shows that they are considerably distant, or their transmitting equipment is damaged." Either way, it implies limited resources and the possibility of conflict over scarce supplies. "The potential for conflict, for competition rather than cooperation, weighed heavily on her mind.

A wave of exhilarating optimism consumed Noah. "They're out there," he exclaimed, his eyes shining with a newfound purpose. We must not ignore them. We must discover their location; they need our help. His youthful enthusiasm was infectious, a potent antidote to the pervasive gloom.

Lily added a vital detail. "The signal...it was intermittent," she explained, "suggested that they may not transmit continuously. We need to act quickly before we lose contact again." The urgency of the situation was undeniable. They could not afford to waste precious time.

Not everyone agreed to venture into the southwest, the compelling circumstances and hope spurred by a weak signal ultimately decided the matter. The prospect of encountering other survivors and of building a larger, stronger community outweighed the inherent risks. The potential for collaboration and mutual support offered a chance to escape the isolating despair that had been their constant companion.

A frantic flurry of preparation filled the days before their expedition. They meticulously gathered supplies, carefully rationing their dwindling food and water. They sharpened their scavenged weapons, tested their makeshift protective gear, and reviewed the scant information gleaned from the fragmented signal. The atmosphere in their subterranean haven was thick with a palpable mixture of excitement, apprehension, and a sense of shared purpose.

They left their haven under the perpetual ash-laden twilight, their hearts pounding with a mixture of anticipation and trepidation. The journey was arduous and filled with unexpected challenges. The terrain was far more treacherous than they expected, a labyrinth of collapsed buildings, treacherous ravines, and stretches of poisonous wasteland. They encountered pockets of hostile scavengers, desperate for resources, forcing them to use their wits and limited weaponry to survive.

Yet, they persevered, fueled by the knowledge that there were others out there, others sharing their plight. The faint hope kindled by the signal acted as a beacon, a compass guiding them toward a shared destiny. They traversed through poisoned landscapes, navigating their way through perilous ruins, their resilience tested to its limits. Every step closer to the coordinates felt like a victory, a testament to their unyielding determination. Driven by the faint hope of establishing contact with others and finding a more secure future, they pressed onward. A quiet anticipation of something more, something better, filled the desolate landscape, which was charged with fresh energy. The faint whisper of hope carried them forward, promising a future where they might no longer be alone. The shadow of the eruption was still long and dark, but now, a small, flickering light shone through a testament to the resilience of the human spirit and the enduring power of hope in the face of utter devastation.

A suffocating blanket of ash and sulfur weighed heavily in the air. Stepping out of the relative safety of their subterranean haven felt like emerging from a womb into a hostile, alien world. The sun, a pale, watery disc behind a perpetual shroud of volcanic dust, cast a sickly yellow light on the landscape, transforming everything into a monochrome palette of grays and browns. The familiar world they had known was gone, replaced by a desolate, almost lunar expanse. Buildings, once proud monuments to human ingenuity, were now skeletal remains, their walls cracked and crumbling, their roofs collapsed in upon themselves like the ribcages of fallen giants. Twisted metal, shards of glass, and the occasional unsettlingly preserved piece of furniture poked out from the ash, grim reminders of a life violently extinguished.

Their initial routed followed the vague coordinated gleaned from the Morse code message, a path leading southwest towards what was once a sprawling residential area. The journey was slow and painstaking, every step requiring careful consideration. The ash, fine as powdered sugar but far more insidious, coated their lungs with each breath, triggering a persistent, hacking cough. They wore makeshift masks fashioned from scavenged cloth and charcoal filters, but even these offered only minimal protection. The ground beneath their feet was treacherous, a shifting landscape of ash and rubble punctuated by hidden cervices and unstable debris. One misstep could lead to a broken leg or, worse, a fatal fall into a hidden chasm.

The silence was deafening, broken only by the occasional crunch of their boots on the ash, the rasp of their ragged breathing, and the distant, mournful cry of a wind whistling through the skeletal remains of the buildings. It was a silence that pressed down on them, a tangible weight that amplified their feelings of isolation and vulnerability. They moved in single file, Ben leading the way, his eyes scanning the landscape for potential hazards. Following Ben, Madison kept her gaze on the ground, searching for edible plants or salvageable resources. Lily trailed behind, her ears constantly alert, listening for any sign of movement or sound that might betray other survivors or potential threats. Noah brought up the rear, his youthful optimism tempered by a growing awareness of the genuine dangers they faced.

As they ventured deeper into the ruins, the landscape grew increasingly treacherous. They encountered collapsed bridges, their rusted girders hanging precariously over gaping ravines. Sections of roads had simply vanished, swallowed by the earth, leaving behind only gaping chasms where once smooth asphalt had run. The weight of the eruption's impact was truly clear here. The entire building was completely gone, leaving only empty spaces filled with rubble. Buildings that remained stood like decaying teeth, monuments to a civilization swallowed by catastrophe. Navigation relied on instinct and what remained of a half-buried street map, meticulously pieced together by Ben from tattered fragments he had found. Even with the map, they got thoroughly lost several times.

The need to scavenger for resources often slowed their progress. Food and water were dwindling, and finding anything edible among the poisonous ash and debris was a matter of luck and careful identification. They consumed what little remained of their stored supplies cautiously, aware that their survival depended on making their limited resources last. They found moments of respite in the scattered pockets of relatively less devastated areas where they could collect rainwater and find edible plants.

The most dangerous encounters, however, were with the scavengers. These were desperate individuals, driven by hunger and the primal urge to survive. They were less organized than a marauding band, more akin to lone wolves, their movements unpredictable, their intentions violent. They tiptoed through the ruins, shadows lurking in the cracks and crevices, their eyes burning with a hunger that surpassed simple food. Their appearances varied, ranging from people in tattered and scavenged clothing to those in makeshift protective suits, their faces obscured by masks or bandanas, leaving only eyes to gauge their threat.

In one particularly tense encounter, they stumbled upon a group of scavengers attempting to loot what remained of a pharmacy. A tense standoff followed a silent exchange of hostile glares, the metallic glint of improvised weapons in the pale light. Fortunately, Ben's quick thinking and ability to negotiate, offering a share of their meager supplies, prevented a violent confrontation. The scavengers, though initially hostile, eventually relented, accepting the offer and giving them a path around the ruined section of the city for their goodwill. This was a crucial moment. It showed to them that not all interactions needed to result in violence and reinforced the important of building connections rather than conflict.

Another harrowing experience unfolded as they passed through what had once been a busy commercial street. A sudden and unexpected collapse of a partially standing building sent a cascade of debris and dust into the air, forcing them to scramble for cover. The initial blast of collapsing debris caught Lily, and Ben and

Noah quickly pulled her from the rubble; her face was pale with shock. Thankfully, she only sustained minor injuries. It highlighted the unpredictable nature of the environment and emphasized the importance of vigilance and teamwork. This close call served as a stark reminder of their vulnerability and the ever-present threat of the ever-shifting landscape.

As the days bled into nights, their journey continued a relentless march through a world remade by the disaster. The nights were harrowing; the darkness amplified by the eerily silent, ash-filled world, punctuated only by the occasional howl of the wind or the distant rumble of shifting tectonic plates. They found shelter wherever they could – in the hollowed-out interior of wrecked cars beneath precarious overhangs of fallen walls, huddled together for warmth and protection. Sleep was a luxury they often went without, their senses constantly on high alert, listening to the creaks and groans of the ruined city, ever watchful for signs of danger.

Despite the hardships, their hope remained a flicker in the darkness. The promise of contact and the possibility of finding other survivors fueled their determination. They pressed on, their bodies weary, their spirits tested, but their resolve unbroken. Although the eruption's long shadow loomed large, they carried within it a small, persistent flame of hope, testament to humanity's indomitable spirit. A faint signal, a mere whisper of hope, had guided them to this desolate place, and its promise kept them moving, one agonizing step at a time, through the ruins of a world lost. Despite the devastating aftermath of the eruption, they pressed forward on them far from over the journey, a testament to their unwavering determination and resilience. The promise of connection, of building a community, fueled their steps. The long shadow of the eruption still stretched across their path, yet the possibility of a future, of hope, beckoned them forward.

Through the perpetual ash-filled sky, the sun, a weak eye, cast long, skeletal shadows across the ravaged landscape. We had been walking for what felt like an eternity; the treacherous terrain slowed the progress not only but also by the unsettling feeling of being watched. The silence, once a crushing weight, now felt strangely charged, punctuated by the occasional rustle of debris or the distant, unsettling creak of a settling building. It was a silence that screamed from hidden dangers and unseen eyes.

Then we saw them.

At first, it was just a flicker of movement – a figure emerging from the shadows of a collapsed building. Then another, and another, until a small group of survivors materialized from the dust-choked ruins, their faces obscured by makeshift masks, their clothes tattered and stained with ash. They were a diverse group, ranging in age from young adults to a weathered elder whose age seemed etched onto their faces by the harsh realities of survival.

Our initial reaction was a mixture of relief and suspicion. Relief at finally encountering other survivors, a tangible sign we were not alone in this desolate wasteland. And suspicion, a natural defense mechanism ingrained in us by the constant threat of violence and the scarcity of resources. Were these people friends or foes? Could we trust them? The questions hung heavy in the air, unspoken yet palpable between us.

Ben took the lead. He raised his hands in a gesture of peace, a slow, deliberate movement intended to convey non-aggression. His voice, when he spoke, was calm and measured, a start in contrast to the frantic pounding of our hearts. "We mean no harm," he said, his words barely audible above the whisper of the wind. "We're just trying to survive, just like you."

The other group responded cautiously, their movements hesitant, their eyes assessing us with a mixture of wariness and hope. A woman stepped forward; her face partially hidden behind a dust-stained bandana. Her voice was raspy, almost lost to the wind, yet it carried a hint of authority. "We've seen other," she said, her words weighed down by a heavy unspoken history. "Not all of them were as peaceful as they seemed." Her words were a cold shower, a stark reminder of the realities of survival in this battered world.

The ensuing conversation was a delicate dance, a careful exchange of information and observations. We learned they called themselves the "Dustwalkers," a nomadic group that had survived by moving from one relatively sheltered pocket to the ruins to another. Their knowledge of the terrain, accumulated through bitter experience, proved invaluable as they led us to a hidden spring, a precious source of clean water tucked away beneath the rubble of a collapsed building.

But trust, even when offered, is a fragile thing. Over the next few days, our interactions with the Dustwalkers were fraught with tension. There were moments of shared laughter, brief respites from the crushing weight of our circumstances, as we shared stories and reminisced about the world that was. There were also moments of conflict, minor disagreements over resources, tensions stemming from differing survival strategies, and ingrained distrust.

One evening, a disagreement over a small cache of canned food nearly erupted into a violent confrontation. The scarcity of resources had stripped away the veneer of civilized behavior, exposing a raw, primal struggle for survival. Madison, ever the peacemaker, stepped in to mediate, reminding both sides of their shared vulnerability and the folly of turning on each other. Her words, though simple, cut through the rising tension, reminding us that cooperation was our only path to survival.

It wasn't just the scarcity of resources that tested our relationships. The psychological impact of the eruption, the trauma of losing everything, and the constant fear of the unknown cast a long shadow over all our interactions. We witnessed firsthand the effects of PTSD, the raw, untamed grief that haunted some survivors, their eyes hollow, their movements jerky and uncontrolled.

The elder of the Dustwalkers, a man they called Silas, shared stories of his past, his voice heavy with loss, his gaze distant and haunted. The eruption caused a mudflow that took his wife, children, and home. He often spent hours sitting quietly by himself, staring out at the desolate landscape, his face etched with grief. His quiet suffering served as a constant reminder of the human cost of the catastrophe.

Then there were the newcomers, survivors who had recently emerged from underground shelters. They were often more aggressive and less adept at navigating the social complexities of this new world, fueled by a desperate need to gather resources and secure their survival.

The days and nights were long, each a struggle for existence. We learned the Dustwalkers had developed their own social hierarchy, governed not by force but by a shared understanding of the limited resources. Their leadership, informal and developing, relied on a consensus-based decision-making process, a pragmatic approach honed by the challenges they faced. We gradually adopted some of their survival tactics and their philosophy of cooperation. We learned to trust them, slowly, hesitantly, but trust.

Yet, the fragile alliance with the Dustwalkers faced constant testing. Rumors of other survivor groups, some violent and predatory, circulated through the ruins. Supposedly, a group known as the "Reapers" was heavily armed and ruthless, preying on weaker groups to claim their supplies. The threat of the Reapers hung over like a dark cloud, a constant reminder of the dangers the group faced.

One night, as the group sat around a meager fire, a desperate plea echoed across the ruins. A voice filled with terror shouted for help. A piercing sound, filled with desperation and pain, tore through the night's silence from the distant cries. We knew, instinctively, that this was not a call for help from a fellow survivor. It was a cry for help from someone who needed protection, and that meant making a tough choice.

The Dustwalkers, initially hesitant, ultimately agreed to join the group. They agreed to help us, not for altruistic reasons, but because of the potential benefits, the potential of increasing their own survival chances. Their decision was based on practicality, and yet, in this shattered world, such practicality was solidarity, a tacit acknowledgement of their shared fate. It was a reluctant alliance, but it was an alliance. The combined strength, even in this dire situation, gave everyone a better chance of survival.

The situation presented to the group was a harsh, chilling reminder of the complexities of human interaction in an environment stripped bare by disaster. In this desolate landscape, even survival, even life itself, was a complex dance of cooperation and conflict, of trust and betrayal, a desperate struggle between compassion and self-preservation. Our encounter with the Dustwalker was a testament to that, a raw, honest reflection of the human spirit, simultaneously broken and unyielding. The shadow of the eruption continued to stretch long across our path, yet we pressed on, our steps faltering, our hope flickering, but our resolve, tempered by the challenges we faced, remained unbroken.

Chapter 17

Normalcy

The distant cries had faded into the unsettling silence of the ruins, but the urgency of the situation remained. Joined with the Dustwalkers, they moved cautiously towards the source of the plea, each step measured, each sense heightened. The air hung heavy with anticipation, and the crunch of our boots punctuated the silence only on broken glass and rubble. The tension was palpable, a tangible thing that weighed down like a physical burden. They were a strange mix, a band of survivors from disparate backgrounds, united only by our shared plight and a growing, tentative trust.

As they approached the source of the cries, a shattered building loomed before us, its skeletal frame a testament to the destructive power of the eruption. Inside, huddled in a corner, were three children – two girls and a boy, no older than ten – their faces streaked with grime and tears, their eyes wide with terror. They huddled together, clutching each other for warmth and comfort, a poignant picture of vulnerability amidst the devastation.

Silas, the elder of the Dustwalkers, kneeled beside them, his weathered face softening with empathy. His touch was gentle and reassuring, a stark contrast to the harsh realities of their surroundings. He spoke to them softly, his voice a balm to their frayed nerves. It was a scene that transcended the usual harsh realities of survival, a reminder of the innate human capacity for compassion, even in the face of unimaginable loss.

Their story was a chilling echo of the disaster. Their parents, they explained in fragmented whispers, had perished in the initial eruption. During the chaotic evacuation, they became separated from their family and found refuge in this dilapidated building. They'd been hiding, scared and alone, for days, living off scraps of food they'd salvaged. Their story was a stark reminder of the human cost of the eruption – children orphaned families torn apart.

Their rescue sparked a turning point. The shared experience and the collective effort to safeguard these vulnerable children strengthened the bonds within the makeshift community. It reaffirmed the necessity of cooperation, of working together to create a safer, more stable environment. We realized that mere survival wasn't enough; the group needed to build a community, a sanctuary where the children and others would feel safe. This rescue was not just a rescue of three children; it was the rescue of collective hope.

The immediate task was shelter and sustenance. The group secured a relatively stable section of the ruins, clearing away debris to create a makeshift shelter. Madison, with her innate resourcefulness, organized the rationing of remaining food supplies, implementing a fair system that prioritized the children's needs. The Dustwalters shared their knowledge of the terrain, leading to additional sources of clean water and edible plants, showcasing profound understanding of this unforgiving environment.

Merely providing basic needs wasn't sufficient to build a community. It needed structure, rules, and a shared vision. Ben proposed the creation of a council, a governing body composed of representatives from both groups. The council decided regarding resource allocation, security, and overall community well-being. The decision-making process was deliberately consensual, reflecting a deep understanding of the need for collective agreement when resources were scarce.

Establishing the council was not without its challenges. The early days were fraught with friction, disagreements over resource allocation, and clashes of personalities. Old survival instincts battled with the emerging need for social cooperation. Arguments erupted, and tensions flared, but the council, while imperfect, demonstrated a willingness to negotiate and find common ground.

It was a messy, often frustrating process, but it was crucial. The council became the cornerstone of our fledgling community, a testament to the ability of humans to adapt and create order even amidst chaos.

Beyond governance, they addressed other crucial aspects of community building. We established a system of tasks and responsibilities, assigning roles based on individual skills and abilities. Some focused on foraging for food and water, others on securing shelter, and some on improving the defenses against potential threats. This division of labor was not only efficient but also reinforced a sense of shared purpose and collective identity. It was a significant step toward creating a more stable, sustainable community.

Slowly, a sense of normalcy, however fragile, emerged. The children, initially withdrawn and terrified, gradually integrated into the community. They played, their laughter echoing through the ruins, a welcome sound that offered a contrast to the omnipresent silence. Their joy was infectious, spreading optimism amidst the despair. Their presence became a powerful motivator, strengthens the groups resolve to create a better future for them.

They documented their experiences, creating a shared narrative, a collective memory of the past, and a foundation for the future. They shared stories, tales of our lives before the eruption, of families and friends lost, and hopes and dreams shattered. The sharing of experiences helped to foster empathy and a sense of shared identity. They were a community forged in the crucible of disaster, bound by shared pain and a collective determination to overcome it.

The process of rebuilding was painstaking, an incremental journey marked by setbacks and minor victories. There were moments of despair when the enormity of the task seemed overwhelming, moments when the weight of the past threatened to crush us under its burden. The presence of the children, their unwavering optimism, and the burgeoning sense of community provided us with the strength to persevere.

They reclaimed a lot of knowledge. Individuals with prior expertise – a former engineer who knew how to construct rudimentary shelters, a retired doctor who offered basic medical care, and an artist who repurposed found objects – stepped forward to share their skills, contributing to the community's overall well-being. This knowledge-sharing became integral to our development, not merely for survival but for fostering a sense of dignity and purpose. We were not simply surviving; we were building.

Yet, the shadow of the past remained a haunting reminder of the fragility of our existence. The memories of the eruption, losing loved ones, and the constant threat of violence cast long shadows over our lives. PTSD was a silent but pervasive presence, affecting some more than others. Group therapy session, led by Madison, provided an outlet for the emotional toll, helping us to process our trauma and find a pathway toward healing.

The community was still in its nascent stage. It was far from perfect, its future uncertain. Yet it was a symbol of human resilience, a testament to our capacity to cooperate, to adapt, and to overcome even the most devastating of circumstances. Our community was a new beginning, a fragile hope blooming amidst the ashes. We were forging a new identity, a new world from the debris of the old, our steps unsteady but our determination unwavering.

The long road to recovery lay ahead, but we walked it together, supporting each other and nurturing the fragile flame of hope in this reborn world.

The rhythmic rasp of Silas's knife against flint echoed the gnawing hunger in our bellies. Our initial reserves, meager even then, were dwindling. Once bountiful harvests orchestrated by Madison were now fading memories, replaced by the harsh realities of dwindling supplies. The vibrant green shoots that had once offered a glimmer of hope were now stunted and brittle under the relentless sun. The clean water source, once a life-giving spring, had shrunk, its flow reduced to a mere trickle.

Food and water weren't the only things scarce. Fuel for the meager fires that fought off the encroaching frosty nights. Cloth to patch torn clothes, protecting us from the elements. Even the simple tools we used for foraging and building were wearing down, their usefulness diminishing with each passing day. Each broken tool represented a potential setback, a slow erosion of our ability to survive.

The initial harmony within the council, so carefully constructed, was fraying at the edges. The fair distribution system. Madison's masterpiece of fairness was now being tested beyond its limits. Arguments, once rare whispers, became more frequent and heated. The division wasn't between Dustwalkers and newcomers, but within each group—between those demanding more and those accepting the need for sharing.

Ben suggested a rationing system based on contribution – those who worked the hardest received a larger share. This proposal, seemingly logical, sparked a fierce debate. The Dustwalkers, with their intimate knowledge of the land, naturally contributed significantly to foraging, but many of the newcomers possessed valuable skills – carpentry, medicine, and even basic engineering – that were equally essential for our survival. How could we quantify the value of these unique skills? How could we ensure that the most vulnerable, the children, didn't suffer?

Madison proposed a different solution – a lottery system, ensuring everyone had an equal chance of receiving the limited resources. This suggestion, while fair on its face, faced immediate resistance. It felt inherently unjust to those who exerted the most effort, who risked life and limb foraging for food and water. The argument intensified, voices rising above the crackling fire, the embers reflecting the anger and frustration in their eyes.

The children, initially oblivious to the adults' growing tension, sensed the shift in mood. Their laughter faded, replaced by a hesitant silence. Their large, dark eyes observed the heated exchanges with an unnerving clarity. The weight of our internal conflicts, it seemed, was settling upon their young shoulders. The sight of their quiet apprehension spurred a sudden wave of guilt among the adults.

Silas, his voice calm but firm, intervened, calling for a temporary halt to the bickering. He spoke of the importance of community, of the shared responsibility that bound them together. He reminded them that the eruption hadn't just taken lives and homes; it had also taken away the ease of living, the abundance they had once taken for granted. He reminded them that their strength lay not in individual achievement but in their collective effort, in their ability to support one another.

His words struck a chord, calming the tempestuous waters. A period of uneasy silence followed, punctured only by the crackling of the fire and the distant sounds of the wind. Then, slowly, tentatively, a fresh path emerged. They reached a compromise—not perfect, but workable. The council agreed on a tiered system, combining elements of both Ben's and Madison's proposals. This system recognized the value of diverse contributions while protecting the most vulnerable.

The new system, however, introduced further complications. Careful monitoring, meticulous record-keeping, and a constantly tested level of trust were required. It meant constant negotiation, an ongoing process of adjustments and compromises. It exposed the deep flaws in human nature – envy, greed, and the relentless pursuit of self-preservation, even at the expense of others.

The council meetings became more frequent, longer, and far more emotionally charged. Accusations flew, friendships were strained, and trust eroded. The shadow of starvation loomed over every discussion, its specter threatening to unravel their fragile community. But amidst the disputes, a certain resilience persisted, a deep-seated understanding that their survival depended on their ability to navigate these challenges together.

Introducing a strict system of accountability added another layer of complexity. They carefully accounted for every piece of food and every drop of water. Intense scrutiny targeted those with access to community stores; officials weighed each action and decision against fairness and community needs. This added layer of responsibility fostered resentment, suspicion, and, sometimes, open defiance.

The artist, previously known for his quiet demeanor and artistic pursuits, became increasingly vocal about his perception of inequity within the rationing system. He argued that his creative work, though intangible, was just as vital to their morale as the tangible contributions of the foragers and builders. His complaints, initially dismissed as the ramblings of a frustrated artist, grew in intensity and found ears among those already discontent.

People initially lauded the engineer for his shelter-building expertise, but later accused him of hoarding materials, prioritizing his own shelter over the community's. The accusations, though ultimately unfounded, caused rifts within the community. The council, despite its best intentions, struggled to resolve the conflict, highlighting the limitations of even the most carefully crafted system in the face of desperate needs.

This struggle for resources extended beyond the material. The psychological toll was also immense. The constant anxiety over survival, the ever-present threat of hunger, and the escalating tensions within the community were wearing down the survivors. Even the Dustwalkers, hardened by years of living on the edge, showed signs of stress and exhaustion. Madison, recognizing the deteriorating mental health of the community, introduced daily meditation sessions, drawing upon ancient survival techniques and spiritual practices to foster calmness and encourage introspection. The sessions proved to be a lifeline, providing a temporary escape from the relentless pressure of survival and offering solace in a world stripped bare.

The scarcity was a crucible, testing the very essence of their newfound community. It revealed their weaknesses, their vulnerabilities, and the deep-seated selfishness that could threaten to unravel even the most altruistic intentions. But it also revealed their strengths – their unwavering determination, their capacity for forgiveness, and their ability to adapt and find common ground, even when confronted by the brutal realities of their situation. Their struggle was not merely a battle for survival but a fight to preserve humanity itself, a testament to the indomitable spirit of cooperation in the face of unimaginable hardship. The road ahead remained long and arduous, but amidst the ashes of their lost world, they were forging a new path, however unsteady, towards a future where sharing and compassion, not scarcity, would dictate their existence.

Chapter 18

The Land

The rhythmic rasp of Silas's knife against flint had become a constant soundtrack to their lives, a grim reminder of their precarious existence. The initial euphoria of survival had long since faded, replaced by a gritty determination forged in the crucible of scarcity. Once a symbol of hope, those vibrant green shoots are now just a memory. The meager harvests barely sustained them, forcing them to explore unconventional methods of food procurement. The ingenious traps Silas had devised, initially supplement their diet, were now their primary source of protein, their effective ess constantly challenged by the dwindling wildlife.

Madison turned her attention to the earth itself. The once-fertile land, ravaged by volcanic ash, now resembled a barren wasteland.

Yet, amidst the devastation, she discovered resilient pockets of life, tenacious plants clinging to existence. These hardy survivors became the basis of their new agricultural endeavors. She experimented with different planting techniques, developing innovative methods to enhance soil fertility and protect vulnerable seedlings from the harsh elements. Using salvaged scraps of metal, she fashioned rudimentary irrigation systems, channeling the dwindling water supply to maximize their yield.

The newcomers, initially reliant on their prior skills, adapted their expertise to the realities of their situation. The carpenter, stripped of his fine lumber, turned to salvaged wood and baboo, constructing durable, if less aesthetically pleasing, shelters. He employed ingenious joinery techniques, learned from necessity to maximize the strength of his creations. The engineer, humbled by accusations of hoarding, poured his energy into developing alternative energy sources. He meticulously salvaged components from destroyed machinery, constructing a crude wind turbine that provided a small but crucial supply of electricity. This electricity powered a newly devised system to pump water from the shrinking stream, a small but vital improvement to their irrigation efforts.

The artist, his spirit initially crushed by the accusations of inequity, channeled his frustration into practical inventions. He transformed discarded metal sheets into tools, creating robust spades and shovels from seemingly useless scraps. His artistic eye, however, was far from dormant. He designed ingenious storage solutions, maximizing the limited space within their shelters and minimizing food spoilage. He even created a series of visual aids depicting the new farming techniques and resource management strategies, making the complex system more accessible to everyone. His art, once purely expressive, now served a crucial practical function, enhancing their collective ability to survive.

Beyond the technological innovations, the community underwent a profound social transformation. The initial conflicts, fueled by scarcity and the fear of starvation, slowly gave way to a newfound appreciation for collaboration. The strict accountability system initially resented, developed into a shared responsibility. Individuals took ownership of their contributions, recognizing the interconnectedness of their efforts. The daily meditation sessions introduced by Madison proved invaluable in fostering this sense of community. These sessions, initially viewed with skepticism by some, became a cherished ritual, providing a sanctuary from the constant pressure of survival and a platform for sharing stories, concerns, and solutions.

Despite its flaws, the tiered system provided a framework for more fair resource distribution. The system increasingly recognized the value of each individual's contribution, however intangible or seemingly insignificant. Building upon the existing system, the community developed a sophisticated system of bartering and exchange, acknowledging the varied skill sets and contributions of its members. The community exchanged artistic creations, once considered frivolous, for food and tools, reflecting the new value placed on creative endeavors.

The children, initially observers of the adults' struggles, became active participants in the rebuilding process. Learning the new agricultural techniques helped them with planting and harvesting. Their small hands performed vital tasks, such as gathering firewood and water. Someone taught them the importance of conservation and the value of every resource. They developed in a keen awareness of their environment, their untutored eyes spotting signs of wildlife and edible plants that often escaped the notice of the adults. Their involvement was crucial not only for their survival but also for the community's collective morale.

The development of new technologies and social structures was a slow, iterative process. There were setbacks and failures. Tools broke, crops failed, and disagreements arose. But each challenge served as a learning experience, strengthening the community's resilience and ingenuity. They learned to adapt, to innovate, and to collaborate, their collective knowledge and experience expanding with each passing day. The community had become a living laboratory, constantly experimenting and refining their approaches, driven by the necessity of survival and the shared desire for a better future.

A deep sense of empathy and mutual understanding resulted from the struggle for survival. The initial divisions between the Dustwalkers and the newcomers gradually dissolved as they shared their knowledge and skills, relying on each other's strengths to overcome common challenges. They had become a genuine community, bound not only by shared hardship but also by a collective commitment to build a better world from the ashes of the old.

The shadow of starvation still lingered, a constant reminder of their vulnerability. Yet, their resilience had grown exponentially. They

had transformed a desolate landscaped into a functioning ecosystem, their innovation a testament to the remarkable capacity of human beings to adapt and thrive even in the face of unimaginable adversity. The road ahead was still arduous, but they walked it together, their steps steady and sure, their eyes fixed on a future where hope, not despair, would dictate their existence. The rhythmic rasp of Sila's knife, once a symbol of their struggle, now echoed the relentless energy of their collective efforts, a testament to their unwavering sprint and innovative solutions to the challenges that lay before them. Their rebuilding was not merely about structures and sustenance; it was about rebuilding hope, faith in each other, and the very fabric of their shared humanity. Despite: In their shared challenges, their strength truly blossomed, despite the far from perfect process. Once fragile and divided, the community slowly transformed, becoming stronger and more resilient—a testament to human adaptation and the bonds forged through adversity.

The dust finally settled, and the first sunrise felt different. It wasn't the warmth of the sun that struck them, but the weight of silence. The rhythmic rasp of Silas's knife, once a constant companion, was now a stark reminder of the work that still lay ahead, a work for grander than simply surviving. Surviving was a given now; building a future was a daunting task before them. A chilling emptiness filled the cleaner air. The vibrant green shoots, painstakingly nurtured, were a fragile promise, a mere whisper against the vast, silent expanse of devastation.

The physical rebuilding was relentless. With a face etched by fatigue, the engineer perfected the wind turbine; its fragile whirring countered the landscape's ominous stillness. The carpenter, hands perpetually raw, crafted sturdy shelters from scavenged materials, his ingenuity transforming debris into havens. But the physical tasks were only half the battle. The psychological scars of the eruption ran deeper than any volcanic fissure.

Madison, ever practical, noticed the growing unease. The communal mediation sessions, once a source of solace, were now punctuated by strained silences, mixed with the occasional outburst of suppressed trauma. The artist painted again, but his canvases depicted not vibrant scenes of nature but stark, haunting visions of the eruption – swirling ash clouds, fractured earth, the desperate scramble for survival. His art became a shared experience, a cathartic release for a community grappling with the collective trauma. The paintings served as a visual representation of their shared journey, a monument to their resilience in the face of unspeakable loss.

Silas carried a weight that was visible in the lines etched deep around his eyes. The constant struggle for survival had exacted a toll on him, and the joy in his eyes, once a beacon of hope, was now clouded with a quiet sorrow. He found himself more often lost in thought, watching the children playing, his face bearing the quiet acceptance of their changed reality.

Surprisingly, the children bore the weight of it all, with resilience beyond their years. They had known nothing but struggle, yet they played amidst the devastation, their laughter a fragile echo against the silence. They helped the adults, carrying water and tending to the small gardens, and their small hands, once accustomed to building sandcastles, were now skillful at building the future. Their games reflected their experiences, building miniature villages from stones and debris, incorporating elements of their shared journey into their imaginative play.

A cold, hard reality had long since replaced the initial euphoria of survival. The community built its success on necessity, responding to an immediate crisis. Now, they faced a more complex challenge: the creation of a sustainable society from the ashes of the old. This involved not only the physical rebuilding of infrastructure but also the creation of a social structure that would encourage collaboration, ensure fair distribution of resources, and address the psychological scars left by the eruption.

The process was far from smooth. Disagreements erupted over resource allocation, sparking tensions that threatened to unravel the fragile peace. Critics intensely scrutinized the tiered system, once a vital framework for resource management, because some felt their skills lacked adequate valuation. Debates raged late into the night, voices raised in the shared desire for fairness and recognition. To ensure everyone was heard and to find compromises, Madison frequently arbitrated. The focus shifted from mere survival to the complex interplay of justice, equity, and community building.

Leadership also came to the forefront. While no one had ever formally declared themselves a leader, Silas, with his experience in wilderness survival, and Madison, with her pragmatism and empathy, naturally took on leadership roles. However, this informal leadership structure was also being questioned and challenged. A new generation of leaders was emerging, individuals who had proven their resilience and skills in the arduous process of rebuilding. The power dynamics within the community developed, creating a new form of governance that was both collaborative and representative. The discovery of gold was the sole positive outcome. With the gold, the groups lived easier lives and had their needs met. Help was not coming from the East soon.

One of the biggest challenges lay in the psychological recovery of the survivors. The shared trauma of the eruption had left deep emotional scars. Nightmares plagued many, and the fear of another eruption was ever-present. Madison organized group therapy sessions where individuals could share their experiences and help each other cope with their trauma. These sessions focused on the artist's haunting paintings, which catalyzed hard conversations and a shared acknowledgment of their collective pain. The process was slow and painstaking, but essential.

The children were not immune to the psychological toll of their experiences. Their imaginative play, while a source of joy, often reflected their anxieties. They would build miniature volcanoes, only to knock them down, recreating the destruction they had witnessed. Recognizing the need for psychological support, Madison started organizing special activities for the children. These activities included storytelling sessions, where they could share their fears and express their emotions creatively. This holistic approach to rebuilding not only addressed the physical needs of the community, but also considered the lasting effects of trauma on the minds of the survivors.

Education also emerged as a pressing concern. The children had lost their formal education. Recognizing the importance of passing on knowledge to the next generation, Madison, with the help of the others, devised a rudimentary education system. This system was based on practical skills like farming, construction, and basic literacy and numeracy. Madison and the others integrated the lessons into the community's daily routines, transforming everyday tasks into learning opportunities. This approach ensured that the children's education reflected the reality of their lives.

But beyond the practicalities of rebuilding, there was a deeper, more profound shift taking place. The survivors, forged in the crucible of adversity, were discovering a profound sense of community, a sense of belonging that transcended the boundaries of individual identity. They had learned to rely on one another, to support each other, to empathize, and to understand each other's vulnerabilities. The bond between them, initially born out of necessity, had transformed into something far deeper, a profound sense of shared purpose and collective responsibility. This shared experience had given birth to a new resilience, a resilience that embraced not only their individual strengths but their collective spirit. The rebuilding process, while difficult, was also a journey of self-discovery and the forging of new identities based on shared experience and a profound respect for shared human dignity.

The future remained uncertain, fraught with challenges that lay ahead. But there was a sense of quiet determination, a shared resolve to overcome any obstacle that came their way. They had looked into the face of destruction and emerged scarred but not broken. Their resilience, their ingenuity, and their unwavering spirit would be their guide as they stepped into the uncertain future, united not only by their shared past but by their shared hope for a brighter tomorrow. Silas's rhythmic knife work symbolized not only survival but also the resilient human spirit, able to forge a new world from the old one's destruction. The rhythmic sound resonated not with desperation but with quiet, steady determination, a testament to their journey, a promise of the future they were now building together.

Silas's knife, once a symbol of survival, now rasped out a quieter rhythm, the steady beat of rebuilding. The community gathered around a crackling fire under the newly constructed wind turbine, looking not at the wreckage of their past but at the nascent structures rising from the ash. A unique quality now infused the air, still faintly smelling of sulfur – a sense of quiet resolve, a shared breath of hope.

Madison, her face etched with the weariness of countless sleepless nights, addressed the assembled group. "We've survived," she began, her voice carrying the weight of their shared experience. "But survival is not enough. We've faced unimaginable loss and seen the earth itself turn against us, yet here we stand. What have we learned?"

A low murmur rippled through the group. Silas, his eyes reflecting the firelight, spoke first. "Preparedness," he said, his voice gravelly but firm. "We were surprised." Next time…next time, we will be ready. We will monitor the seismic activity, improve our warning systems, and have evacuation plans in place. We'll create a network of communication that can withstand any disruption." He gestured towards the newly erected communication tower, a testament to their commitment to preparedness. Its antenna, reaching towards the star-dusted sky, symbolized their hope for a more secure future.

The carpenter added, "Cooperation. We built this together. We shared our skills, our resources, and our strengths. Without that unity, we wouldn't be here today." He looked at the children playing nearby, their laughter a fragile melody in the evening air. "They are the future, and their education will be a cornerstone of our future preparedness. We'll learn from our mistakes and ensure that each generation is better prepared than the last." He pointed to the makeshift schoolhouse, constructed from salvaged materials, its simple structure a symbol of their shared commitment to knowledge and education.

The engineer, his face illuminated by the glow of the turbine, spoke of resilience. "We faced seemingly insurmountable odds. The scale of the devastation was overwhelming. Yet we didn't give up.

We innovated, we adapted, we persevered. Our resilience is not merely physical; it's a testament to the power of the human spirit." He spoke of the ingenious solutions they had devised, the repurposing of materials, and the innovative use of limited resources. The turbine itself was a symbol of that inventive spirit, a testament to human ingenuity in the face of adversity.

The artist's paintings now depict not just the destruction but also the rebuilding, resilience, and hope, which shared his perspective. "Art is a mirror to our souls," he said, his voice quiet but powerful. "Through our art, we process our grief, our trauma, our hope. It helps us understand our shared journey, and it allows us to express the inexpressible. The art of rebuilding is as important as the physical reconstruction." His paintings now served as visual records of their journey, a testament to the emotional resilience of the community. The colors were bolder now, richer, reflecting the increasing strength of their spirit.

The discussions continued late into the night. They talked about the challenges of resource allocation, the need for a fairer system, and the importance of maintaining harmony and cooperation. They analyzed their successes and their shortcomings, acknowledging the mistakes made and vowing to learn from them.

The tiered system, initially designed for efficient resource management, had caused some friction. They agreed to revise it, ensuring that everyone felt valued and fairly compensated for their contributions. They implemented a system of rotating responsibilities, ensuring that everyone could take part in decision-making processes.

The informal leadership structure, previously defined by Silas's practical skills and Madison's empathy, began to grow. Representatives from various skill sets and viewpoints formed a council. This council wasn't based on authority but on collaboration consensus-building, and a shared commitment to the well-being of the community.

The psychological well-being of the community remained a priority. The nightmares persisted, and the fear of another eruption lingered, but they were learning to cope. Madison's group therapy sessions continued, providing a safe space for sharing and healing. The artist's paintings served as a powerful tool for processing collective trauma, allowing them to confront their fears and experiences in a creative and therapeutic ways. The children's games, once reflections of their trauma, shifted. Their play incorporated elements of rebuilding, creativity, and hope, demonstrating their adaptation and healing process.

Despite its rudimentary nature, the new education system thrived. The new system: The new system removed the classroom's confinement of learning. The rebuilding process provided children with a hands-on learning experience. Learning practical skills ensured their survival and the community's sustainability. Learning about sustainable farming, basic construction, and resource preservation was part of their education. They learned about their shared history and the importance of preserving knowledge for future generations. They learned about teamwork, cooperation, and problem-solving, transforming adversity into an invaluable learning experience.

The community established a system of rotating responsibilities, ensuring that every member had opportunities to contribute according to their skills and interests. This fostered a sense of shared ownership and responsibility, further strengthening the community bond. Experienced members created a mentorship system to guide younger members, effectively passing on knowledge and skills.

Their new society wasn't perfect. Conflicts still arose, and disagreements still flared, but they were learning to resolve them constructively, with respect and understanding. They had established a transparent system for addressing grievances, ensuring fairness and equity in their interactions. They had learned that conflict wasn't necessarily destructive; it could be a catalyst for growth and improvement, an opportunity to learn and adapt.

Above all, they learned the profound importance of community. The bond they shared forged in the crucible of disaster transcended mere survival. The people powerfully showcased human resilience and strength in the face of adversity, a testament to the enduring human spirit when people unite. It was a lesson that emerges when people come together in the face of adversity. It was a lesson that extended beyond their immediate reality, a lesson that they would carry with them into an uncertain future.

The future remained uncertain. The land remained scarred, a reminder of the catastrophe. But there was hope. A hope rooted not in naïve optimism but in the lessons learned, in the resilience gained, in the enduring power of the human spirit. The rasp of Silas's knife was now a quiet rhythm, a steady beat, a constant reminder of their journey, a testament to the new world they were building together from the ashes of the old. The sound now held not just the echo of survival but the promise of a brighter, more resilient future built on the foundations of shared experience, empathy, and unwavering hope. It was the sound of a community reborn, stronger, wiser, and forever bound by the shared experience of rebuilding a world.

Everyone who formed the community led a hard but happy life. Since the eruption, no one came back out west to live. It was like the old days when people came west in buggies. This land was special to the survivors, and this land is where they will continue to live.

Madison and Noah married and had four children. Those children grew up to be community leaders. Ben also stayed and married a woman from Silas's group. Ben was the community architect and developed running water and waste removal. He formed roads and the infrastructure for the power and electrical systems.

Mr. and Mrs. Henderson lived a long, happy life, both passing in their sleep. The Henderson's were very active in establishing the school system and created the educational programming for all the children. They even came up with the first football league that was the most important event in the town.

Chapter 19

Long Term Survival

The sun, a pale disc in the perpetually hazy sky, cast long shadows across the altered landscape. Years had passed since the eruption, years had passed since the eruption, years measured not in seasons but in the slow, agonizing crawl of regrowth. Where once stood vibrant forests, now stretched desolate plains, scarred and pockmarked by volcanic flows that had solidified into a surreal, otherworldly landscape. Twisted, blackened tree trunks, skeletal remains of a bygone era, clawed at the sky like the fingers of some ancient, petrified beast. The air, though cleaner now, still held a subtle tang of sulfur, a constant, low-level reminder of the cataclysm that had reshaped their world.

The once-fertile valleys, buried under feet of ash and pumice, were slowly yielding to the relentless march of nature. Hardy pioneer plants, tenacious survivors, pushed their way through the debris, their vibrant greens a stark contrast to the monochrome palette of the surrounding devastation. These were the first tentative steps in the long process of ecological recovery, a testament to the resilience of life itself. But the changes were profound and far-reaching. The eruption had not only altered the physical landscape but also reshaped the global climate, triggering erratic weather patterns and plunging much of the world into a prolonged period of volcanic winter.

The rivers, once lifeblood of the region, now flowed sluggishly, choked with sediment and debris. Their waters, once crystal clear, were now a murky brown, carrying the ghosts of the past. Now murky brown, the lakes, once crystal clear, carried the ghosts of the past. Now choked with ash, the lakes, once shimmering mirrors of the azure sky, had lifeless gray surfaces. The animals, those that had survived the initial blast, had adapted to or perished, their populations decimated, and their habitats irrevocably changed. An unnerving silence replaced the familiar songs of the forest, punctuated only by the occasional screech of a surviving bird or the rustle of a small mammal foraging in the sparse undergrowth.

Once vibrant hubs of activity, the human settlements were now mere ghosts of their former selves. Something reduced the meticulously planned villages and carefully constructed towns to rubble. Only the most resilient structures remained, scarred and battered but still standing, a testament to human ingenuity and perseverance. The people, scattered and dispersed, had begun the slow, arduous process of rebuilding their lives, their communities, and their world.

Silas surveyed the progress. Once a symbol of hope, the wind turbine now stood as a testament to their long road to self-sufficiency. Diligent maintenance and repair of the solar panels ensured a vital energy source, powering the new homes and the rudimentary irrigation system, slowly reviving patches of land. The communication network, painstakingly established across the ravaged landscape, was the lifeline connecting the scattered communities, fostering cooperation and enabling them to share resources and information.

Madison dedicated herself to the community's mental and emotional well-being, despite her countless sleepless nights. The group therapy sessions continued, offering a safe space for processing the trauma, the grief, and the shared loss, the artist, his canvases now displaying a palette of hope, documented their journey, their resilience, and their ongoing struggle to rebuild their lives. His art was more than just a reflection of their experiences; it was a tool for healing, a catalyst for connection, and a powerful reminder of their shared humanity.

The children, once traumatized by the eruption, were now learning to navigate this new world, adapting to the challenges and embracing the opportunities. Their play was no longer shaped by fear and uncertainty; it was a celebration of resilience, a testament to their capacity for hope. They were learning the skills of survival, self-reliance, and community building. Their education, though rudimentary, was vital, providing them with the knowledge and skills needed to thrive in this changed world.

Initially efficient, the new societal structures were now adapting to the community's growing needs. Acting as a bridge between the various settlements, the council—formed years ago—facilitates cooperation and resource allocation. The emphasis was on transparency, equity, and shared responsibility. The challenges were immense: dealing with the sporadic aftershocks, managing limited resources, ensuring fair distribution of food and supplies, addressing lingering psychological trauma, and maintaining a sense of unity and purpose in a world forever changed.

Ecological changes presented a formidable challenge. Unpredictable weather patterns, caused by the altered climate, disrupted farming and led to sporadic droughts and floods. Despite: Despite slowly yielding to nature, the volcanic ash still threatened agriculture and water quality. Dwindling resources and habitat loss made adaptation difficult for the animals. The slow process of ecological recovery was far from guaranteed. The long-term effects of the eruption on the global climate remained a source of uncertainty and concern.

The once-vibrant ecosystems, reduced to a state of devastation, were gradually undergoing a process of transformation. New species, opportunistic survivors, were colonizing the barren landscape, creating new ecosystems that were unlike anything seen before. The landscape was dynamic, constantly changing, a constant reminder of the earth's power and the fragility of life itself.

Challenges, far more subtle yet equally daunting, faced the community that had survived the initial cataclysm. Recurring nightmares, anxieties, and depression lingered like the psychological scars of the eruption. The constant threat of further volcanic activity, though statistically less likely, remained a constant source of apprehension. The scarcity of resources, the unpredictability of the weather, and the challenges of establishing a sustainable society in a post-apocalyptic world tested their resilience at every turn.

Despite the persistent challenges, a spirit of determination and hope prevailed. The community had learned the importance of collaboration, adaptability, and resilience. They had adapted their farming techniques to the ash-laden soil, developed innovative methods for water conservation, and established a sustainable system for managing their resources. They had learned to live in harmony with the changed landscape, using the geothermal energy generated by the volcano to power their homes and businesses. Years after the eruption, the landscape remained a stark reminder of the catastrophe, but it was also a testament to the resilience of both nature and humanity. The survivors, scarred but not broken, continued their journey of rebuilding, adapting, and forging a fresh path in the face of adversity. The rasp of Sila's knife, the quiet rhythm of rebuilding, resonated not just in the sounds of their daily tasks, but in the unwavering hope that filled their hearts. It was a sound of perseverance, a testament to the enduring human spirit, a symphony of survival echoing in the heart of a transformed world. Despite an uncertain future, they stood united, ready, and determined to face any challenges together. The ashes of the past had become the foundation of their new future, a future built on resilience, cooperation, and the unshakeable belief in the power of hope.

The fresh sounds of their rebuilt world – the rhythmic clang of metal, the rasp of saw on wood, the hum of geothermal generators – formed a soundtrack to a life rising from devastation's ashes. Nestled in the lee of the now-dormant volcano, the village stood as a testament to human ingenuity and resilience. Homes constructed from salvaged materials and innovative designs clustered together, creating a sense of community of shared purpose. The once-straight lines of streets had yielded to a more organic layout, following the contours of the land, weaving through the newly established orchards and vegetable patches.

The children played a game of tag amongst the newly planted fruit trees, their laughter echoing through the valley – a sound that had once been almost unimaginable. They were a generation born into the shadow of the eruption; their understanding of the world shaped by the scars that marred the landscape. Their untamed energy and vibrant play showed childhood's enduring power. Their games were not just about fun; they were a vital part of their education, a practical application of survival skills. They learned to identify edible plants, to navigate the treacherous terrain, to recognize the signs of changing weather.

Madison watched the children from afar. The deep lines around her eyes spoke of sleepless nights spent tending to the community's emotional wounds, of countless hours dedicated to fostering resilience and healing. Her work as a counselor had strengthened; it was no longer just about addressing the immediate trauma of the eruption but about navigating the ongoing challenges of a world forever transformed. She created a curriculum focused on mental wellness that was integrated into the community's daily life. Regular group sessions, mindfulness exercises, and creative art therapy formed the core of her program, helping the community build emotional resilience and navigate the daily stressors of their altered reality. She knew the psychological scars ran deep, the nightmares persisted, the anxieties a constant companion. But she also saw the growth, the strength, the remarkable ability of the human spirit to adapt and heal. Post traumatic stress disorder was still running rampant.

Silas continued to survey the progress of the irrigation system. The meticulous network of pipes, carefully laid across the volcanic terrain, channeled the precious geothermal water to the fields. His understanding of engineering, gleaned from years of tinkering and experimentation, had proved invaluable. He was the community's engineer, their problem-solver, the one who could coax functionality from salvaged parts and make something new from the wreckage of the old. His leadership was not one of command but of collaboration, of sharing his knowledge and skills to empower others. The success of the irrigation system, a testament to his dedication, guaranteed their food security, and this instilled a sense of stability in the community. He had found purpose and satisfaction in rebuilding their world, brick by brick, pipe by pipe.

The new societal structures reflected the challenges and triumphs of their experiences. The council, initially a pragmatic necessity, had grown into a genuine expression of democratic ideals. Transparency and equity were paramount. They decided collectively, valuing everyone's voice. The community understood the importance of collaboration and shared responsibility. The community encouraged individual initiative, but always within the framework of collective well-being. They had learned that survival in this new world depended on their capacity to work together, to support each other, to share resources and knowledge.

The artist, once consumed by the despair of loss, found a new purpose in chronicling their journey. His raw expression of grief and trauma powerfully developed into a testament to human resilience. The transformed landscape, tenacious pioneer plants, rebuilt homes, and smiling children's faces were all captured on his canvases. His art served a purpose beyond mere historical documentation; He displayed his art in public spaces, not as a gallery exhibit, but as a shared narrative, a tool for community engagement, strengthening their collective identity.

Although: The shadow of the past, though, never fully vanished. Not easily forgotten were the eruption, loss of loved ones, and near societal annihilation. Despite their infrequent and less intense nature, the sporadic aftershocks constantly reminded everyone of the volcano's dormant power. The volcanic winter, although gradually abating, still left its mark on the climate, leading to unpredictable weather patterns. The lingering ash in the soil, though gradually being improved through careful soil management techniques, still posed a challenge to agriculture. These constant reminders of the fragility of life instilled a profound respect for nature and an understanding of the limitations of human control.

But the community had learned to adapt, to live in a state of cautious optimism. They had developed a deep appreciation for the interconnectedness of life and a sustainable relationship with the transformed environment. They had created a society based on resilience, collaboration, and a shared commitment to building a better future. Their new normal was not merely a survival; it was a flourishing, albeit one built on the foundations of a shared past. The vibrant colors of their newly established farms, the confident smiles of their children, the hope reflected in the eyes of their elders — these were all testaments to their remarkable capacity to not only endure but to thrive, to transform loss into strength and build a future from the ashes of the past. Their story was not one of mere survival but a powerful narrative of resilience, innovation, and the enduring strength of the human spirit. The world had changed, but they had changed with it, forging an alternative path, a new normal, in the mountain's shadow that had reshaped their world.

The first memorial was a simple affair, a ring of stones gathered from the riverbed, each smooth surface worn by the relentless flow of time, mirroring the slow, steady healing of the community. Each stone represented a life lost, a silent testament to the devastating power of the eruption. The stones bore no names and lacked elaborate carvings. Their simplicity was their power: a quiet acknowledgement of the immense loss, a space for silent reflection, a place where tears could fall unseen and grief could find solace. As the days turned into weeks, the circle of stones grew, becoming a secret space, a focal point for communal remembrance.

Later, a more ambitious project took shape – a living memorial, a vibrant orchard planted on the slopes of the volcano overlooking the village. Each tree was a tribute, carefully chosen for its resilience and beauty. Within its branches, they saw the promise of new beginnings, a symbol of lif3e springing forth from the ashes of destruction. The orchard wasn't just a visual tribute; however, it was a source of sustenance, a tangible reminder of the community's ability to transform loss into nourishment. The act of planting the trees, of nurturing their growth, became a collective therapy, a shared process of healing. Each sapling, carefully planted into the volcanic soil, represented a shared hope, a silent promise to honor the lives lost by embracing the future.

Madison took the lead in designing a structured approach to the community's grief, recognizing that unprocessed trauma could linger, poisoning the potential for long-term well-being. She incorporated grief rituals into their daily life, understanding that grief wasn't a linear process but a cyclical one that required acknowledgment and acceptance.

People held regular memorial gatherings, not as somber events, but as opportunities for shared reflection and catharsis. People shared stories of those lost, celebrating the lives lived and legacies left behind, not dwelling on the sorrow. These weren't just tales of loss but of love, strength, and the indelible mark each individual had left on the hearts of those who remained.

These gatherings incorporated elements of creative expression, an understanding that artistic outlets could help unlock bottled-up emotions. Children painted vibrant portraits of their loved ones on canvases made from recycled materials, their colorful expressions a poignant juxtaposition to the subdued tones of the memorial stones. Adults crafted intricate sculptures from volcanic rock, their rough textures subtly mirroring the raw emotions they sought to express. These creations became treasured possessions, personal reminders of the deceased, and symbolic representations of their ongoing legacy. The artist, initially struck silent by his own grief, found his voice again, not just through painting the landscape but through capturing the essence of this shared mourning, transforming raw emotion into art that the community could both understand and share.

Silas was busy expanding his engineering skills to constructing a memorial that reached beyond the immediate village. He designed a network of trails that wound through the reformed landscape, showcasing the resilience of nature but also commemorating specific sites of loss. The trails became not just paths for walking, but symbolic journeys. Each turn and incline represented a stage of grief and healing. He placed small, sturdy benches at vantage points along the trails, each offering a panoramic view of the valley, a place for quiet reflection, a chance to contemplate the journey of life and loss. These were not simply places to mourn but to reflect, to appreciate the beauty that remained, and to re-engage with the world. Silas even restored fresh water and sewage with the use of the trails.

The new social structure prevented anyone from grieving alone. A support network, meticulously woven into the fabric of the community, provided a lifeline to those struggling. Regular check-ins, coupled with easy access to counseling sessions, ensured that everyone had a support system capable of addressing their unique needs. The council took the initiative in developing programs specifically designed to address the needs of children and adolescents who had witnessed the eruption, implementing regular group sessions facilitated by trained counselors and using play therapy and other child-appropriate methods to unlock and process their traumatic experiences.

As a complex symbol, the volcano represented both destruction and creation. The fear had lessened, replaced by a grudging respect. The community's survival hinged on understanding its power and its unpredictable nature. Regular seismic monitoring became integral to their daily life, a constant reminder of the ongoing risk and a demonstration of their commitment to staying informed and safe. They created a comprehensive emergency preparedness plan and practiced regularly, ensuring the eruption's lessons remained relevant. They were not only preparing for potential future eruptions but also honing their capacity for adaptation and communal resilience.

They couldn't erase it. The memorials powerfully symbolized resilience and community spirit. The new village, thriving in the shadow of the dormant volcano, was a testament to their transformation – a living embodiment of the profound lessons learned from the loss and the transformative power of shared grief, shared healing, and a shared commitment to a future where remembrance and optimism could coexist. They wove stories of the past into the fabric of their present, reminding them of life's fragile beauty and the need to celebrate it daily. The vibrant colors of their farms, the laughter of their children, and the quiet strength of their elders – all bore testament to a community that had not only survived but had redefined the very meaning of thriving. They had faced the abyss, stared into the heart of loss, and emerged, transformed into a vibrant community bound by the memory of what they had lost and the unwavering hope for what they could still achieve.

Chapter 20

The Future

The first tremor, barely perceptible, sent a ripple of unease through the newly planted orchard. It was a faint shudder, a ghost of the cataclysm that had reshaped their world, but enough to remind them of the precariousness of their peace. The laughter of children playing amongst the blossoming trees momentarily stilled, replaced by a hushed expectancy. Old Man Hemlock, his face etched with the wisdom of a lifetime spent observing the volcano's moods, raised a hand, silencing the anxious whispers. He pointed a gnarled finger towards the mountain, its peak shrouded in a wisp of cloud. "She breathes," he said, his voice raspy but calm, "and we must remember to breathe with her."

The fragile peace wasn't merely the absence of violence; it was a delicate balance maintained through constant vigilance and unwavering community spirit. The council, composed of representatives from all segments of the society, met regularly, not just to address immediate concerns but to expect future challenges. The shadow of the volcano loomed large, both literally and metaphorically, reminding them of the ephemeral nature of their newfound stability. They knew that the dormant giant could awaken at any moment, and preparedness was no longer a luxury but a necessity for survival.

Maintaining order requested a constant calibration of pragmatism and compassion. Silas, with his engineering mind, had devised a system of early warning signals, a network of sensors extending far beyond the village, designed to detect even the subtlest seismic shifts. These sensors weren't just technological marvels, they were a tangible representation of the community's commitment to preparedness, a symbol of their collective resilience. The village received the information immediately; this triggered a pre-arranged response plan, meticulously practiced through regular drills. These drills, while initially met with apprehension, had become a ritualized aspect of their lives, a constant reminder of the need for collective action and coordinated response. However, the most formidable challenge wasn't the potential for another eruption but the subtle erosion of trust that sometimes threatened to undermine their unity. Whispers of dissent surfaced, fueled by exhaustion, frustration, and the lingering trauma of the past. Some questioned the council's decisions, others felt overlooked or ignored, and a few individuals openly expressed a longing for the days before the eruption, oblivious to the destructive forces that had nearly annihilated them. Madison, with her understanding of human psychology, recognized the danger of these simmering resentments. She started a series of community dialogues, creating a safe space for the airing of grievances and the reconciliation of differences.

These dialogues weren't merely meetings; they were carefully orchestrated events aimed at fostering empathy and understanding. They began with shared meals, breaking bread together, a symbolic gesture of unity. Then, guided by Madison and her team of counselors, the participants engaged in facilitated discussions, using storytelling and group activities to help process their emotional turmoil. These sessions, far from being confrontational, allowed individuals to express their anxieties and frustrations without judgment, facilitating catharsis and encouraging a renewed sense of shared purpose. Continuing to thrive, the art therapy program, started after the eruption, provided a creative outlet for the community's emotional expression.

Significant challenges also arose from the ever-changing environment. The volcanos' eruption had altered the landscape, creating new challenges to their livelihoods. Volcanic ash had significantly affected the fertile land around the volcano. Silas, alongside other skilled members of the community, devised innovative farming techniques to overcome this challenge. They experimented with different soil amendments, adapted irrigation systems, and cultivated crops that were resilient to the unique conditions. This innovative approach not only ensured food security but also fostered a shared sense of ingenuity and collaboration.

Effects from the eruption extended beyond the immediate surroundings. The eruption severely disrupted surrounding ecosystems, affecting wildlife populations and the availability of natural resources. The council, in collaboration with environment scientists who had joined their community, implemented a comprehensive plan for ecological restoration, focusing on reforestation, water management, and wildlife conservation. This project became a symbol of the community's commitment to sustainability, a testament to their understanding that the health of the environment was intrinsically linked to their own well-being.

Maintaining security was also a constant concern. Limited resources existed, and deep physical and emotional scars from the past remained. The community established a volunteer patrol system composed of individuals trained in basic self-defense and emergency response. The community did not intend this system to be overly authoritarian, but to foster a sense of collective responsibility for safety. Every member of the community played a role in maintaining security, recognizing that peace required an ongoing collective effort, not simply relying on a centralized authority.

Despite their best efforts, however, challenges remained. Erratic weather patterns threatened their crops and livestock. The

psychological scars left by the eruption manifested in unexpected ways, with some individuals suffering from recurring nightmares, others experiencing bouts of acute anxiety, and a few exhibiting symptoms of post-traumatic stress disorder. The counseling sessions, while immensely helpful, couldn't fully address the depth and complexity of the trauma experienced. Madison continued to advocate for additional support, lobbying for outside help and developing innovative therapeutic approaches to address the specific needs of the community.

Yet, amidst these ongoing challenges, a sense of hope persisted. Living memorial orchard continued to flourish, a symbol of the community's resilience. The children, though scarred by their experiences, demonstrated an extraordinary capacity for resilience, their laughter echoing the newly built homes, a testament to their capacity to find joy amidst adversity. The trails built by Silas remained not only pathways through the landscape, but also pathways to healing, providing spaces for individual reflection and communal gathering.

Fragile peace was not a guarantee of uninterrupted tranquility; it was a testament to the community's shared commitment to perseverance and to their unwavering belief in the possibility of rebuilding and healing. It was a daily, hourly struggle, a constant negotiation between the scars of the past and the hope for the future. The volcano remained a powerful symbol, a constant reminder of the power of nature and the precariousness of existence. Yet, in the shadow of the dormant giant, a new community emerged, resilient, creative, and eternally bound by the shared experience of loss and the shared hope for a future where remembrance and optimism could finally coexist in harmony. The whispers of the wind through the orchard trees carried not just the faint rumble of the volcano, but also the soft murmur of hope, a testament to the strength and resilience of the human spirit. Their journey was far from over, but they continued to move forward, step by step, towards a brighter, more hopeful tomorrow.

The sun dipped below the horizon, painting the sky in hues of orange and purple, a breathtaking spectacle that momentarily distracted from the ever-present shadow of the volcano. As darkness descended, the village hummed with a quiet energy. The aroma of wood-smoke mingled with the sweet scent of the blossoming orchard, a comforting blend that spoke of resilience and renewal. Inside the community hall, the rhythmic strumming of a guitar accompanied the soft voices of the storytelling circle.

This nightly ritual, a cherished tradition since the rebuilding, provided a space for sharing experiences, both happy and harrowing, a testament to the community's commitment to healing and remembrance.

Tonight's stories focused on the future, the plans for expanding the orchard, and the ambitious project to build a geothermal power plant, harnessing the volcano's energy for sustainable living. These weren't just idle dreams; they were meticulously planned initiatives developed through countless meetings, discussions, and compromises. Silas, ever the pragmatic engineer, presented detailed blueprints of the power plant, his voice brimming with cautious optimism. He meticulously outlined the safety measures, the environmental impact studies, and the long-term sustainability strategies. His presentation was not a mere technical explanation; it was a hopeful declaration, a tangible expression of the community's unwavering belief in their ability to build a sustainable future.

Madison, ever attuned to the emotional currents of the community, followed Silas' presentation with a heartfelt speech that emphasized the importance of collective effort and unwavering hope. She spoke of the children, their laughter echoing through the newly painted trees, a symbol of the unbroken human spirit. Their wisdom guided the community through its trials and tribulations, she explained. She spoke of the shared sorrow but, most importantly, of all the shared dreams that bound them together. Her speech wasn't solely about rebuilding; it was about rediscovering their collective identity and forging a stronger sense of belonging in the face of unimaginable adversity.

The discussions that followed were as vibrant and diverse as the community itself. Some expressed anxieties about the ambitious project, highlighting the potential risks associated with harnessing the volcano's power. Others voiced concerns about the environmental impact, questioning whether their interventions would disrupt the delicate ecological balance that was slowly being restored. They did not dismiss these concerns; The community understood that progress should not come at the expense of their hard-won sustainability and safety.

The community's commitment to education played a crucial role in their long-term vision. A small school built from salvaged materials had become a hub of learning, nurturing the next generation of engineers, scientists, doctors, nurses, and community leaders. The curriculum wasn't just about academic subjects; it incorporated practical skills like sustainable farming, basic engineering, and disaster preparedness. This holistic approach aims to equip children with survival tools and foster their sense of ownership and responsibility for their future.

The ongoing ecological restoration project continued to be a source of pride and hope. Promising results emerged from reforestation efforts, as new trees thrived on the volcano slopes. The wildlife, once decimated by the eruption, was gradually returning, its presence a silent testament to nature's tenacity and the community's diligent conservation efforts. The council, in collaboration with the visiting scientists, had developed a comprehensive monitoring program, watched the recovery of the ecosystem and adapted their strategies as needed.

Growing, the living memorial orchard became a symbol of remembrance and renewal. Each tree represented a life lost, a memory cherished, a lesson learned. The orchard wasn't just a collection of trees; it was a living testament to the community's resilience, a tangible symbol of their unwavering belief in the power of life to overcome adversity. As the trees grew taller, their branches reaching toward the sky, so too did the community's hope for a brighter future.

Beyond the immediate surroundings, the community-maintained contact with the outside world, receiving vital supplies and sharing their experiences. Their story had spread, capturing the imagination of people around the globe and inspiring others with their resilience and their commitment to rebuilding. This external support not only provided valuable resources but also strengthened their sense of community, reinforcing their belief in the power of human connection to overcome adversity.

Despite their triumphs, the shadow of the volcano remained a stark reminder of the precarious nature of their existence. Regular seismic monitoring remained a crucial aspect of their lives, a constant reminder of the potential for future eruptions. However, this constant vigilance wasn't a source of paralyzing fear; it was a motivating factor, driving them to create a society that was prepared for any eventuality.

The community's journey had been fraught with challenges, but their collective spirit had remained unbroken. They had learned to adapt, innovate, and collaborate, forging a stronger, more resilient community in the wake of a disaster. The stories they shared around their nightly fires weren't merely tales of survival; they were stories of hope, resilience, and enduring power of the human spirit.

The construction of the geothermal plant represented more than just a technological achievement; it was a bold statement of intent, a beacon of hope in a landscape still scarred by the eruption. It was a testament to their ingenuity and their unwavering belief in their ability to harness nature's power for the betterment of their lives. The designers incorporated innovative safety features into the design, minimizing risks from volcano energy use. The community understood that their future depended on finding a sustainable balance between innovation and responsibility.

The long-term plans extended beyond infrastructure; they encompassed cultural and social development. Creativity, education, and a strong social fabric were the major priorities. The community recognized that the reconstruction process was not just about physical rebuilding, but also about healing the deep emotional wounds left by the eruption. The storytelling circle, the art therapy programs, and the community dialogues continued to play a crucial role in this healing process.

The survivors understood that their experience was unique, but their resilience and determination were universal. Their story became a symbol of hope, a reminder that even in the face of unimaginable adversity, the human spirit could endure, adapt, and ultimately thrive. Their journey was a testament to the power of collective action, the importance of community, and the enduring hope for a brighter future. As they looked towards the horizon, they saw not only the majestic peak of the volcano but also the promise of a new dawn, a future built on the foundations of resilience, collaboration, and an unwavering belief in the enduring power of hope. The wind whispered through the orchard, carrying with it not just the memory of the eruption but also the promise of a future where the human spirit could not only survive but truly flourish.

~The End~

Afterward

Depending on who you ask, Yellowstone is overdue for an eruption. Because an eruption by a super-volcano can affect life on earth, Yellowstone is unique, as it is on the mainland of a populated country. Yellowstone is not the only super-volcano, but it is the most active. There are certain parts of the parks the periodic close because vents will expel steaming water and endanger visitors. When considering these facts, it's easy to understand why Yellowstone is one of the most monitored volcanos in the world.

The massive ash fall will cut those near Yellowstone off from the rest of the world. Taking refuge in a cave, a deep cave is probably one way to survive during an eruption. It is also not uncommon to find that civilizations lived in the caverns deep in the caves found in the west. There are stories of Montezuma and other Aztecs hiding their gold in the West, buried in caves. Blind Frog Ranch in the Uintah Basin of Utah is reputed to be one such hiding place. This ranch has found bead sites and other antiquities found there. A

History Channel show features this ranch. There are many stories and lores of gold hidden in the tunnels of the north and southwest. As to yet, they all remain unfound.

●●●

Bonus Excerpt from the Soon to be released
UTOPIA

Prologue

Year: 2010

It was freezing out, and it was also late. Her parents really let her stay up way past her bedtime. Delilah and her aba were sitting outside in Adirondack chairs, sipping on hot cocoa ima made. Because it was so cold outside, ima wrapped everyone in her quilts.

Nights like tonight were really special. Lila waited all year for these nights. Even in summer, these nights are fun, but something about the cold air made them perfect. The night sky somehow seemed crisp.

They would sit outside and point out the constellations and worlds. Was there life? What was their lives like? Did they have to go to school too? Did they have school bullies waiting for them? Were they sitting outside now, looking at our world and wondering what we were like?

Aba would tell Lila to bring him home a rock when she went out into space. It amazed Lila that he really thought she would roam the universe! When Lila went to sleep, she often dreamed about those worlds and the things she could learn!

Lila dreamed of becoming a doctor. She enjoyed studying medicine. Most importantly, Lila loved learning. Her mind was like a sponge, keeping the lessons she learned in school. In her mind, she could picture the books she read. Lila could actually see the pages when she closed her eyes! A photographic memory, it was called. It came in handy when Lila had a test. She did not know how she got that talent, but Lila thanked Hashem for helping her out with her schoolwork.

Lila worked her way through school. Her ima told her she should take a year and become a nurse. She could easily find a nursing job that would continue to pay for her schooling, and she was right.

For some unknown reason, Lila wanted to go to Vanderbilt University. She still thinks back to the day she received her acceptance letter. It was strange leaving home. Ima packed Lila with lots of quilts to take to Tennessee with her. When Delilah Dweck graduated college, she was a medical physician and also had a doctorate in genetics. Now it was off to become an astronaut.

Ima and Aba passed on and she had no other family who was going to crack a bottle of champagne when she took off.

Astronaut training was the most intense activity she could conjure up. Aba did not tell her all that she would go through.

To become an astronaut, there was initial training. That included almost every kind of science: geology, meteorology, astronomy, physics, spacecraft systems, International Space Station Systems, learning to speak Russian, Flight training on T38 jets, Survival training, weightlessness simulations, robotics training, then, and only then, could you advance to mission specific training.

When you reached mission specific training, you were still not an astronaut. That just allowed you to reach the second stage of training. The second module comprised specialized mission trainings. That could mean anything. Experiment preparations and contingency planning, which was a polite way of saying what to do when the shit hit the fan. Also, international collaborations. How to work with astronauts from other countries.

By now, the prospective astronaut is still not an astronaut, but can advance to the third module and that involves the training facilities.

This third module is definitely not for the faint of heart! It involves training at the Neutral Buoyancy Laboratory at Johnson Space Center, the Virtual Reality Laboratory, T-38 training, Space Vehicle Mockup facilities, GARN facilities, Sonny Carter Training Facility, which contains the largest pool in the world, 6.2 million gallons.

Ten hours of underwater training equals one spacewalk. And once you are done with these trainings, you are still not an astronaut. There is one training left: 1,000 simulation approaches before landing the shuttle. Once you achieve that, then, and only then, my friend, you are at last, an astronaut.

The requirements to be a NASA astronaut are four requirements:

- Be a U.S. citizen;
- Possess a Master's degree in a STEM field. A doctorate is the best;
- Earn 1,000 hours of flight training, at a minimum;
- Pass a flight physical exam

There is a height requirement of no taller than 6'3". Pilots must be a minimum of 5'4'.

Being a female astronaut comes with its own special turmoil. NASA's official policy prohibits pregnancy in space. NASA tests women for pregnancy regularly in the 10 days before launch. Most female astronauts eagerly take the hormones to avoid menstruation in space. Of all the female astronauts Delilah has worked with, they were thankful for the hormones. No one admits to having a period in space; whether it has happened remains unknown.

Delilah Eve Dweck was beyond ecstatic when she received her official email from Celestia X, the private contractor that does the space missions jointly with NASA. Celestia X, selected her to be the mission specialist physician for the Mars Magellan mission. The press made humor of her middle name of Eve. She will also be the first woman to be on Mars, even though there will be six other women. There are 14 astronauts, or the first Mars settlers, on this mission.

This is not only a one-way space mission to Mars, but the astronauts view this mission as the making of a new country, new world. Each voyager has the same thoughts, starting off a new world. These 14 souls would have meetings getting to know each other and discuss what they would like to see in the new world.

Many of these "getting to know you" meetings took place away from NASA and Celestia X.

Delilah had been on two trips to the International Space Station under Expedition 72. She was doing research on genetic sequencing and pharmaceutical manufacturing. The entire trip up to space and back to earth, Lila thought of her parents. Her aba would have been her biggest cheerleader.

The one thing the residents of earth did not think about in this space mission was about its successors. No one really thought about the implications of this one-way trip. Part of the study is populating a new planet. There were seven men and seven women for a reason.

Besides natural conception, NASA thought of everything and included 60,000 fertilized blastocyst embryos. The bean counters at NASA determined that to have 100% natural genetic diversity, there needed to be a gene pool of 10,000 to 40,000 people. Instead of trying to ship that many people to Mars, eight-day-old blastocysts were the answer. Any woman can carry a donor embryo and the genetic makeup remains separate from the egg and sperm donors. Each woman can attempt a natural pregnancy, and they encouraged this, but after one or two natural conceptions, they will need to use donor embryos. It was Delilah's job to keep track of the genetics to make sure there was no inbreeding. Ironically, someone had hoodwinked the public. The entire Mars mission is a huge science experiment and the creation of a new race, Martians.

Chapter 1

The Magellan Crew

NASA and Celestia X handpicked the crew for the Magellan. No one knew the criteria NASA and Celestia X used for selecting the crew. Mostly, the astronauts were unmarried, except for the Captain Aris Thorne. He is married and has three children. Delilah often wondered what he told his wife or what she thought. Captain Aris's wife would come with the children on the second flight. There would be at least a ten-year separation until they would reunite. That is forever in space timing.

The other crew of the Magellan were:

Dr. Delilah Dweck, who was a mission specialist, physician, and geneticist.

Dr. Laura Hoover, assistant commander and co-pilot.

Dr. Jacob Stern, mission specialist and an astrobiologist. He went to Vanderbilt University with Delilah. They are old friends.

Dr. Meera Sharma, mission specialist and Astro agriculturist.

Dr. David Jackson, mission specialist, structural engineer.

Dr. Amanda Benson, mission specialist, engineering and systems specialist.

Dr. Jonathan Smith, mission specialist and geologist.

Dr. Julie Dorn, mission specialist, physicist, and chemist.

Dr. Stanley Gross, mission specialist, astrobiologist.

Dr. Mark Redding, mission specialist, life sciences and backup pilot.

Dr. Rosemary Davis, mission specialist, structural engineering.

Dr. Ryan Fleming, mission specialist, chemist.

Dr. Lisa Lombard, mission specialist, physicist and chemist.

After the public learned the identities of the astronauts bound for Mars, many interview requests poured in. Because of all the publicity, the astronauts stayed in NASA quarters and focus on the mission.

There was little free time and the free time, each wanted to say goodbye to friends and family, packing the meager possessions they could take, and looking at favorite spots on earth for the last time.

Delilah spent her time sitting in the Adirondack chairs at her parent's home, looking at the night stars, wrapped in one of her ima's quilts. Her packing was going to be light: her family photos, her ima's recipes, and her ima's homemade quilts. She had no boyfriends and had no social life. Going to see one final movie theater movie and having a buttered popcorn was her last hurrah.

The other astronauts were planning going away parties, but if the truth was told, she was closest to the other astronauts. They've spent years training together, locked in a space station at the bottom of an immense pool and in jets together. The one thing she wanted was to have a prayer put in the Wailing Wall. Going to Israel to do it was not an option, but a Chabad rabbi was doing it for her. Lila joked with the rabbi that she was setting up the first Chabad on Mars.

The crew were all friends, texting one another, and even came to each other's going away parties. If truth be told, Lila couldn't wait to blast off on the new chapter of her life. The crew were chomping at the bit because they were going to wait until they were on their way to Mars, when they would start outlining their new world. Each made lists of things they wanted different in the new world. One major one was a cashless society. There would be no money, no wages, everything communal. Not a communist society, but with one in nature and family. Like it or not, they were all now a family. The nine-month flight time was going to be spent hammering out a sort of Constitution without the formality. Each astronaut was taking their job seriously and embraced the role they were now in.

Chapter 2

Launch Preparations

The air crackled with a nervous energy, a palpable hum vibrating through the steel and concrete of the Kennedy Space Center. Not the hum of machinery, though that was present in abundance, a symphony of whirring servos, hissing hydraulics, and the low thrum of power conduits – but a deeper, more human vibration. It was the collective anxiety, the shared anticipation, the weight of human hope pressing down on every shoulder in the vast complex. The Magellan, humanity's ark to a new world, stood poised on the launchpad, a colossal testament to ambition and audacity, its gleaming white hull reflecting the Florida sun.

Days bled into weeks leading up to this moment. They painstakingly checked and re-checked each system, component, and tiny screws, analyzing and re-analyzing each one. The meticulous preparations had been a brutal dance between precision and urgency, a relentless pursuit of perfection against the ticking clock. Fourteen astronauts underwent a relentless schedule.

They were more than astronauts; they were pioneers, founders, the seeds of a new civilization.

Dr. Aris Thorne, mission commander, a veteran of multiple space missions and a renowned astrophysicist, found himself drawn to the observation deck. From his vantage point, the entire launch facility was visible—a sprawling complex, a city devoted to space exploration. Below, the sprawling infrastructure throbbed with activity. Technicians swarmed over the Magellan like industrious ants, making last checks and calibrations. Engineers huddled around glowing screens, their faces illuminated by the flickering light, monitoring a thousand different systems simultaneously. The sheer scale of the operation was awe-inspiring, a testament to humanity's unwavering spirit of exploration.

He thought of his family – his wife, Elara, a celebrated botanist who had helped design the Magellan's hydroponic systems, and his two children, Lyra and Orion, were too young to fully comprehend the enormity of their father's undertaking. He had spent months preparing them, trying to explain the importance of the mission, the responsibility that rested on his and his crew's shoulders. He'd shown them pictures of Mars, the rusty deserts and towering volcanoes, and they'd imagined building homes among those alien landscapes. But the reality of leaving them, of potentially facing a one-way journey, was a weight he carried in his heart, a silent burden shared by every astronaut.

The emotional farewells had been heartbreaking, a poignant tapestry of tearful embraces, whispered promises, and silent goodbyes. Each astronaut carried with them a piece of Earth, a collection of cherished memories and the love of their families, a silent anchor to their home world. Pride and profound sorrow filled the families as they watched their loved ones, hope and trepidation warring in their hearts, from the designated viewing area.

Immense pressure, a suffocating blanket of responsibility, permeated every aspect of the crew's lives. The weight of expectation rested heavily on their shoulders – the hopes of humanity, the future of the species, literally, rested upon the success of this mission. Failure was not an option. This was not just about planting a flag on another planet; it was about establishing a new home, a sustainable haven for future generations. The 60,000 fertilized blastocyte, nestled securely within the Magellan's cryogenic chambers, represented not merely a gene pool, but the very fabric of a future society, a future humanity.

The meticulously planned launch sequence was a marvel of human ingenuity. A countdown, echoing in the crisp morning air, marked the culmination of years of planning, trillions of dollars invested, and countless hours of dedicated effort. Each second ticked by with agonizing slowness, a prelude to the cataclysmic release of energy that would send the Magellan hurtling towards Mars. The roar of the engines, a guttural growl of power, shook the very ground beneath their feet, a testament to the immense thrust required to overcome the Earth's gravitational pull.

They dedicated the next few weeks to the meticulous procedures necessary for a successful Mars mission. The astronauts went through a series of checks and preparations, constantly monitoring the spaceship's status. They made sure that all the systems were in order, the life-support mechanisms operating smoothly, and the navigation systems working correctly. The sheer volume of tasks was immense, and the crew were constantly busy, meticulously testing and re-testing every aspect of their systems.

Remarkably, the voyage began with uneventful phases. The routine of daily life aboard the Magellan settled into a comfortable rhythm – regular meals, exercise routines designed to combat the effects of prolonged weightlessness, periods of scientific research, and, of course, periods of rest. Yet, beneath this veneer of routine, a deeper current flowed – the anticipation of the unknown, the excitement of discovery, and the silent weight of responsibility. A new future, where the crew would test the limits of human ambition and the resilience of the human spirit, was the destination of the crew's course to Mars. Humanity's vulnerability in the face of cosmic grandeur was underscored by the vast, unforgiving emptiness of space and the immense task ahead. The launch marked only the first step of a journey that would change human history forever. The genuine challenges were yet to come.

Technicians fitted each astronaut with adult diapers as they dressed in their spacesuits for takeoff. At least, no one will ask to pull over for a bathroom break.

The shuttle team tightened their belts so tightly that breathing was difficult. Their tight straps gripped them in their seats. In fact, it was so tight the astronauts were immune to vibrations.

The launch team finished their work, wished the astronauts Godspeed and locked the Magellan. The astronauts were waiting for the countdown to begin. No matter how many times a person has been in space, the ride never gets easier. Sometimes it is even harder going back to space again because you know what the ride is like.